DEADLY DREAMS

DEADLY DREAMS

by
Gerald A. Schiller

INTERCONTINENTAL PUBLISHING

ISBN 1-881164-81-0

Cover Design: Dawn Schiller, Nightwatch Graphics
Back Cover Photo: John Torrey
Design and Typography: Sans Serif, Inc.

To Esther, Lisabeth, and Greg, my severest critics—
and biggest fans, and to Joe Steinberg,
a good friend who has helped make
many of my projects become reality.

1 ❖
Nightmare

IT WAS HAPPENING AGAIN. The mist. Struggling to find her way. Then the corridor. Endless. White. Sterile. The white doors all locked. Finally one opens. The room is cavernous—dim—a hum—tiny flashing lights. And then . . .

She can see it. Beds along the wall. A hospital ward? Figures lie under plastic sheeting. Their faces distorted, grotesque. Beside them machines hum and buzz, hum and buzz, tiny lights flash. Red. Yellow. Green monitors with pulsating curves.

She moves closer.

Under the sheeting the faces are contorted, the bodies writhe in spasms. Are they alive?

Suddenly a noise at the end of the corridor.

She moves toward it.

A large door is ajar. Voices reverberate beyond it. She moves hypnotically to the voices. Fearful, yes, but unable to go back.

The door swings open. The light is blinding. Huge operating room lights—a figure on a table—surrounded by surgically gowned figures.

Their voices echo as they work. What do they say?

"Spleen."

"Liver."

"Kidney."

Their bloody hands slice into the body. Each organ is removed. Then. . .

They see her. They stop. All look at her. Behind the masks the piercing eyes are all she can see.

Terrified, she turns.

But the door behind her is locked.

She is in bed. Her bed. Her nightown is soaked. Slowly she runs her hand across her breasts, under her arm, down between her legs. Her sweaty gown clings to her like a second skin. She turns to the table. The digital red glow says 4:26, the colon pulsating. She pulls herself up and moves to the window. The street below is quiet. A cat slowly slinks across, hunting.

The nightmare had returned. She thought it was gone, but it had come back. How long had it been? Two weeks? Three? And it was always the same. The hospital ward. The surgeons. The locked door and no escape. And it always ended that way.

Denise Burton peeled off her sweaty nightgown and moved to the tiny bathroom. She looked at herself, almost naked, in the doorlength mirror. Not bad for a woman who was approaching forty. She had kept her figure. But why? Vanity? She turned and ran her hand down her buttocks. It's been a long time since a man's hand did that. Her hand slid under the elastic of her panties and down between her legs. And that. She stopped and moved to the shower. As she turned the old porcelain knobs the blast of water roused her, and she slipped out of the panties and let the hot water caress her skin.

Denise Burton worked hard to maintain her looks. She was thirty-seven years old, dark haired, and extremely well-proportioned. Denise would not have stood out in a crowd or been mistaken for a movie star, but she was attractive. At five feet three she was hardly model material, but her body was trim and in good shape. Her eyes were deep brown and flashed when she was excited. Since divorcing her husband (a divorce that she once said "had been made in heaven"), she had resisted the temptation to let herself go. She saw too many divorcees who got fat (apparently substituting eating for sex) and let their wardrobes deteriorate (feeling "why bother?").

Twice a week Denise went to aerobics classes and, while she couldn't keep up with the pace of the twenty-somethings, she worked out to exhaustion religiously, kept an eye on her diet (resisting that constant temptation to order dessert) and devoted one day a month to shopping for clothes.

And though she looked younger, the pickings were slim indeed. Marikem Industries, where she worked, had a vast stable of young, attractive secretaries, and the unmarried, eligible men pursued those young ones, and the older, divorced men were likewise after those same young things. Her dates were few and far between and, though she maintained hope, each new birthday seemed to push the possibilities further away.

As her six-year-old Chevy pulled off the freeway and eased into the San Fernando Valley traffic, she was still thinking about the dream. Maybe she could find a doctor to give her something to help her sleep. Maybe she needed a psychiatrist, but why? Dreams. Didn't they mean things? Did this one symbolize some hidden fear? Something from her childhood? Who knows? Maybe I should read a book on dreams. Maybe I really need Dr. Freud.

Marikem Industries was in Chatsworth, a part of the San Fernando Valley normally known for its upscale homes. The plant sat on a rise that commanded a view of the houses and shopping centers north of the Ventura Freeway. It was a large complex occupying four acres with over a thousand employees. And, ironically, Denise—like a good percentage of Marikem's employees—wasn't totally sure just what they did there. Chemical engineering, she was told. Military contracts—she guessed from the reports she dealt with. To her it was just a job. She had answered an ad, gone for an interview, impressed the interviewer with her intelligence and computer skills, and gotten hired. The pay was decent so she stayed.

Denise had a good attendance record, worked quickly and efficiently, and was a dependable employee. After a year and a half she was put in charge of her typing section. Her supervisor quickly recognized her intelligence and skills. In another two months she even had a minimum security clearance. Now Denise directed the labors of six people who worked at the word processors.

She was very early this morning. Nothing like being shaken awake at 4:30 to make sure you get to work on time. There it was. The huge Marikem Industries complex up on the hill. It was nice not fighting downtown traffic and driving out to the valley every day. It was a nice place to be too. Pleasant people. Pleasant work—at least most of the time.

She moved into the line approaching the guard gate. Her purse was on the seat beside her and she fumbled for her pass. Don't know why there's so much security in this damn place. Pictures. Fingerprints. ID Cards. She was at the gate before she found it. The old guard waited patiently—she must remember to get that card out earlier. Finally she had it, and extended it out the window. He gave a perfunctory look and waved her on. Some security. Probably could have showed him my driver's license.

Denise worked busily supervising the others, organizing their work, apportioning the assignments. There were reports and surveys and endless data about this experiment and that development. When the work load was heavy, she pitched in and hit the keyboard with the others. And she was a fast typist—always had been. But she always had been happier pounding at the electric typewriter. Computers? She had been forced to learn them. She caught on fast and now she could word process like the best of them. But she still preferred the old electric. She was working busily when a voice interrupted.

"Hey!"

Across the room Edie Pulaski was calling.

"What is it?"

"Break time."

"Oh, I didn't even notice. Let's get some coffee."

Edie Pulaski was a talker. She was short, pert, blonde, and spirited—but she was an incessant talker. She talked to fill in the gaps of silence if there were any. She talked about herself, about anybody she knew, and even about anybody she didn't know. She asked questions like a defense attorney and never seemed content with a short answer. She was thirty-one and had never been married—she said she was having too good a time to spoil it. But of late Denise had noticed that she talked more and more about subjects like commitment, settling down, and her biological clock.

Denise liked her—to an extent. They went to aerobics class together, shopped together frequently (Denise thought Edie had good taste and could provide honest criticisms of any outfit she might try on). They talked to each other on the phone when they were lonely. But when Edie started her incessant cross-examination, Denise wanted to scream. She could accept Edie's litany of her dates and the bizarre relationships she got herself into. But when she began her questioning of Denise, it just got to be too much.

They stood sipping their coffee beside the row of vending machines lined up along the hallway. It wasn't very good but there really wasn't enough time to get down to the cafeteria before lunch so they sipped the vile stuff and complained about it.

"You look kinda tired." Edie was eyeing her. "Heavy date?"

"Fat chance."

"Well, nothin' was on TV last night. Trouble sleepin'?"

"Yep. The nightmare is back. I thought it was gone for good, but back it came. I was up at 4:30. Couldn't get back to sleep."

"Maybe you should try some tranquilizers—or sleepin' pills —or somethin'."

"I hate taking medicine, but I guess I'm gonna have to get something. I'll call a doctor tomorrow. Do you think I should—well—see a shrink?"

"I dunno. If all else fails. We do have a health plan y'-know. Let the company pay for it."

"Not a bad idea."

They were back at their desks now and Denise was pitching in, sharing the workload, oblivious to her surroundings. The light touch on her arm startled her.

Lawrence Hillman stood there. He was in charge of the section. A short, balding, officious man of fifty or so, he was impressed with his own limited authority and obviously working toward bigger and better things. Hillman had been put in charge of their section, Research Reports and Data, about a year ago and worked his staff hard. He was a fair man but a go-getter and sometimes his typists felt he drove them a bit too relentlessly. He always seemed in a hurry, eager to get the work out, eager to impress his superiors with his department's skill and competence. And he relied on Denise.

"Miss Burton, I can't get any of the messengers. They're all busy. Would you do this for me?"

He was holding a pile of folders and looking very frustrated.

"They need all this material on the sixth floor right away and I just can't get anyone to take it for me. Room 605."

Denise was wondering why he couldn't do it himself, but decided to run his little errand. She could use a break from typing.

She took the pile of folders and headed for the elevator. The building was quiet, and she went up quickly. She had a little trouble finding the room. Apparently the room numbering was not well marked up here. It took several twists and turns along some corridors to find 605 but she delivered the folders with minimum problems and headed back to the elevator. But for a moment she couldn't remember exactly which way she had come.

She retraced her steps and turned down a hallway but it was the wrong one. Suddenly she stopped. The white walls, the white doorways. Sterile. She had been here before. Slowly she moved along the empty hall. Yes, she had been here before. It was exactly like her dream.

2 ❖
Déjà Vu

IT WAS MORE THAN STRANGE. It was shattering. And it wasn't just the color of the walls and doors. It was an aura. Something about this hallway was identical to her dream. What was it? She had to find out. There was no one in sight, so she began to move down the hall. Should she try a door? She moved to the right. There was nothing on the door but a number, but she was drawn to it. 644. She reached for the handle.

Suddenly a hand touched her arm. Startled, she turned.

She was staring at a very good-looking man. He must have been in his thirties. He wore a white lab coat and carried a clipboard. At first glance Denise was both surprised and impressed. He had sandy hair, blue eyes that penetrated her gaze, and a very business-like air to him. She was surprised that someone had appeared in this empty hallway. And impressed that it was someone so attractive.

"I didn't mean to startle you, but this is a security area."

She noticed a security ID on his coat pocket. She could see his picture and was trying to read the name.

"Miss, you can't be in this area without a maximum security ID."

"Oh, sorry."

"Can I help you?"

"I was just—having some trouble finding the elevator, that's all."

"Well if you turn left over there and then right, you won't have a problem."

"Thanks."

She turned and moved down the hall. As she reached the end and started to turn, she looked back over her shoulder. The man was opening a door. She tried to see inside, but quickly it closed.

The film was over. As the credits rolled, Denise dozed. TV always did that to her. She missed some of the most fascinating movies. There must be something about the television screen that hypnotized you. How had the damn thing ended? She hoped Edie was watching or somebody else at work. She'd have to find out tomorrow.

She pushed the remote switch and the screen went blank. I can do without the eleven o'clock news tonight. Maybe I can get some sleep—if the damn nightmare leaves me alone.

And that corridor she'd been in today. Could it be the one from my dream? I've never been up on that floor, have I?

Denise stared at the blank screen and went over those few moments when she stood in that hallway. It must have been a coincidence. There have to be hundreds of halls like that one. But there was something about it that reminded her of the dream. What was it?

The phone purred at her. She always felt that phones shouldn't purr. They used to ring.

"Denise?"

There was an all too familiar voice in a hushed whisper on the line.

"Denise?"

She should have guessed. Who else would call at eleven at night. The one, the only.

"Denise, this is Donald."

Donald Burton. The world's champion loser. The greatest excuse for a man since who? She couldn't think of anyone to compare him to. Donald Burton. He had been her husband for three miserable years. The divorce was easy. But getting him out of her life was impossible. There was always something. And here he was again.

"Yes, Donald."

"Denise, you've got to help me. I'm in trouble—"

"I've heard it all before, Donald. Over and over—"

"No, this is serious. They'll kill me this time."

"Come on. Cut the drama. How much do you need?"

"It's not money. Please. I'm at Twelfth and San Pedro. You've got to come —-right away. If they find me, I'm a dead man. Honest, Denise."

"Donald, it's after eleven. I had a lousy night last night. I really would like to go to—"

"I think it's them! Please, Denise. I won't ask for anything else—please—"

There was the click and he hung up.

Damn. Damn. Damn. This is too much. I'm not married to him anymore. Let them kill him. Whoever they are. I'm not Donald's keeper. He probably deserves it.

She was still cursing him as she put on her coat and headed out the door to her car.

3 ❖
The Loser

SHE LIVED IN NORTH HOLLYWOOD, not a very prestigious area, but comfortable and convenient to get to work on the freeway. Getting downtown was easy too, so—now and then when she could afford it—she went to a show, heading into town to the Music Center, but always dreading the drive through the city's center. She always parked under the theater complex (even though it cost more) and when the show was over, drove hurriedly away from the area. She hated the sight of downtown Los Angeles, and this was just one more reason why Donald's late night call had annoyed her.

Now she was driving through the dilapidated war zone of the inner city. Her built-in middle class fear and revulsion came to the surface as she watched the sickening night time drama on the streets around her. The winos lying in the doorways, the druggies making their furtive contacts in the shadows, an occasional whore keeping an eye out for an expensive car that might be cruising looking for a late hour pickup. And every now and then, a police car ignoring the whole sordid picture.

At Twelfth and San Pedro she pulled to a stop. The area looked deserted. It was a warehouse district with apparently no one around. The buildings were dark, and little could be made out but the scrawled white graffiti across the sides of the old buildings.

Suddenly there was a tapping at her window. Startled, she turned to see a dark figure gesturing frantically at her.

It was Donald. A very different Donald. Even in the dark

she could make out the disheveled, unkempt hair, the stubble of beard, the ratty clothes. He might have been one of the winos she had just passed if she hadn't recognized him.

She reached over and unlocked the passenger door and he quickly moved around the car and got in. His movements were like a cornered animal, constantly looking behind him, cowed in fear, broken in spirit. This was worse than the Donald she had seen at his lowest ebb. She felt compassion for this poor wreck of a man, but the hatred and annoyance she felt were still there.

"God, you look awful."

"I know I do, Denise. Look, can we get out of here? Somebody might be watching for me."

"This cab driver would like to know where to."

"Oh, anywhere. Just drive around for a few minutes, huh. Just to make sure I'm not being followed."

She pulled the car away from the sidewalk, thankful to be getting out of this area, and headed north to the freeway to take her to more comfortable surroundings, the homes and lawns of the city's middle class

"I can't thank you enough for this, Denise. You really saved my ass."

"You're welcome, I guess. So what happened this time?"

"It's a long story."

"You might as well spill it. This may be a very long evening."

"Well, I was the middle man in a—well a little—transaction."

"A drug deal, right?"

"Sort of. I was the one to deliver the stuff. And get the money. I'd get ten percent of the deal. I knew the guys involved. But I got screwed by the buyer. He had his buddies with him and they took the dope and never paid. So I'm stuck in the middle. The seller thinks I've crossed him and wants the cash. But I don't have it. And now he's after me. Believe me, Denise, he'll kill me. This guy means business."

"So what am I supposed to do? Go out and raise money so you can pay some sleazy drug dealer?"

"No, I'd never ask you for that."

She drove along the darkened street. A few people waited on the sidewalk for a late bus. The liquor stores and fast food joints flashed their gaudy inducements to stop and buy.

"Denise. I need a place to hide. Just for a day or two. If you could put me up on the couch—"

"Absolutely not."

"Just a day or two, Denise. I promise to be out of your hair—out of your life after that."

"I think I've heard that one two or three dozen times."

"I mean it this time. I do, honest."

Denise glanced over at the wreck of what had once been her husband. If she just dumped him on the street, she would be rid of him. How would he end up? Dead, in all likelihood, eventually. Then she would really be finished with this albatross that dragged her down and involved her in his sordid life. But the guilt. That she would never be rid of. She'd live with that for the rest of her life. How could she go on with her life knowing she'd been responsible for the death of someone else? Yet it wasn't her fault. He was an adult, thinking human being, responsible for his own actions. She chuckled.

"What's funny, Denise?"

"I'm thinking of what a sucker I am."

She pulled her car onto the freeway on-ramp.

A shower and shave made a big difference. She even had some of his old clothes. She had kept them to wear when she did cleaning and car washing. He looked better in them than she did. She had warmed up some leftover food and as the new, clean Donald moved into the kitchen there was more than a hint of what she had once seen in him. He was, undoubtedly, a good looking man. As he gobbled up the meat loaf and peas, and sopped the gravy with bread, she remembered what those few good years had been like.

He was a a kind and gentle man but living with him had been hell.

"I've put some sheets and a pillow and blankets on the couch. You should be comfortable. But dammit, Donald, don't get too comfortable."

"You don't have to worry, Denise. I'll be gone—in two days."

"You better be."

The Donald Burton she had met that day so many years ago was different. He was a man who had charmed an almost innocent Denise Porter. He had to. Their cars had collided as he pulled out of a driveway and they both stood alternately eyeing each other and staring at the mutilated fenders and cracked headlamps. Both cars had suffered about the same and both were probably driveable. But Denise was angry. She had been invited to a party and was expectantly primed to meet some "interesting young men" (as the hostess had put it). And now she stood on a street corner—her car smashed—her evening rapidly ebbing away. Should she just get the guy's name and take off?

She looked at him. He wore jeans and a tee-shirt with some rock group's name emblazoned on it. But he was hardly a teenager. He must have been at least thirty or so. His black hair was disheveled and he was out of breath. Most of all, he was very distressed by the accident he had caused and very apologetic.

"I'm sorry, Miss. I admit it *was* my fault."

"You're damn right it was."

"Look, I've got to be somewhere in a few minutes and—"

"So do I."

"Well, I hate to admit it, but—if my insurance company finds out about this—well—they might cancel me—"

"So?"

"Look, I'm willing to get your car fixed. I know a good body shop—"

"How can I be sure of that?"

He had pulled out his wallet and was flashing all the ID he had: credit cards, membership cards, bank cards. It all looked okay to Denise so they exchanged phone numbers and went their separate ways.

Denise's party turned out to be a major dud. The hostess kept trying to introduce her to all the weirdos she was trying to avoid, and all the genuinely interesting men were accompanied by women who kept wary eyes on them throughout the evening. But the next day when Donald Burton did call and they met to take the car to the body shop (a noisy, smelly little hole-in-the-wall in East L.A.), and then ended up having lunch together (in a noisy little Mexican restaurant which turned out to be excellent), the relationship between Denise and Donald began.

He *was* a charmer. There was always a little gift: flowers, a favorite book, a poster for her apartment. And his taste was good—he bought things she would have bought herself— if she hadn't thought they were minor extravagances. Almost from the beginning, they seemed on the same wave length.

He didn't take her to expensive places. His funds were modest (at the time he worked in a book store). There were movies and lunches and marvelous walks in the park. And there were museums and even the zoo. Denise discovered— with Donald—a whole new dimension to a city she thought she knew.

Both of them were adventurous. Denise—ever since childhood—had been fearless, always eager to try something new. Her parents lived in constant fear she would never make it out of childhood and indeed she had her share of skinned knees and elbows, broken bones from falls out of trees, even a mild concussion when she took a dare from her schoolmates and walked along the edge of the roof of a two story house— at the age of nine—and fell headlong into some bushes.

As a grown woman she still did her share of fearless activities. She had tried snow skiing, scuba diving, even bungee jumping (on one occasion). She liked the thrill of it all. When Denise had time off, there was always something that she hadn't tried and she was eager to experience it—at least once. With Donald she loved to hike the mountains of Southern California. He had trouble keeping up, but dutifully, huffing and puffing, kept pace, generally well behind her. They hiked to elevations where snow covered the ground and threw snowballs at each other. On one occasion Donald had slipped in the snow and almost plummeted down a mountainside. Denise had grabbed him and hung on until he regained his footing. The experience made him warier at least, but their hiking continued.

After six months they were married. The idyll lasted perhaps another year. Then Donald started getting involved with people she didn't like—types who promised to help him get ahead but who really contributed to his downward spiral. The second year became the year of hell. Denise knew then it was not going to get any better. But she stayed on hoping. Finally she realized it was an impossible situation. She left him and filed for a divorce. He pleaded with her but did not contest it. When the divorce was final, she thought it would be over. But with Donald there was no end.

She undressed slowly. In the next room was a man. A man she had slept with many times. A man who was a caring, often passionate lover. Remembering some of those blissful moments, the fun they had had as they tumbled in bed, kissing, caressing, stroking each other's skin. Donald's sensual tongue, his gentle, though insistent fingers. The remembrance excited her. She stood, naked, staring at the door. On the other side of it was a man who had been responsible for so many exciting moments. She moved to the door. Slowly, she opened it.

Across the room on the couch Donald lay, snoring in exhaustion.

She closed the door, put on her nightgown, and crawled into her solitary bed.

4 ❖
Bad Guys and Good Guys

DONALD WAS STILL ASLEEP as she showered, dressed and headed out the door. He looked so peaceful lying there. He reminded her of the kids she supervised that summer at camp. Hellions by day; angels as they slept. Poor Donald. He really was a kid. The trouble was—he kept getting involved in things with the big boys. And he always suffered.

And she suffered too.

The weird characters he brought home—always because they had deals he was involved in—seemed to get more and more unsavory. After their divorce, several of these former creeps kept calling her, wanting to go out. One even came over to the apartment—unannounced—and started to grab at her. A swift kick in the groin informed him she was not interested and he left her alone from that point.

But Denise decided it was time to take some steps to protect herself. She enrolled in the Y's self defense classes and learned some techniques that would help her if another of Donald's friends should get too affectionate. And with a rash of rapes and attacks on women in her neighborhood, these were skills she felt would definitely come in handy—just in case.

She saw an ad in the paper about shooting lessons and spent three Saturday afternoons learning—a bit—about firearms. On an indoor firing range Denise was instructed in handling, loading, and firing handguns and the appropriate safety measures when using one. But she couldn't bring herself to buy a gun in spite of the instructor's assurance that she was capable. She felt uncomfortable having one around the house—having heard all the horror stories about accidental shootings. So though she learned the techniques of using one, she never bought a weapon. Her friends told her she had wasted her money, but Denise felt it was information she might use some day—and maybe she might bring herself to purchase a gun sometime in the future. Who knows?

But there had been no nightmare that night. In spite of Donald and his late night phone call, she had slept well. Maybe his troubles kept her mind off those dreams. Maybe.

At work things went their usual mundane way all morning. Organizing the work for the typists, making sure it all got done, chatting with Edie. Lunchtime came as a welcome relief. She sat with Edie at a table in the company cafeteria, eating her fruit salad, cottage cheese, rye crackers, and sipping her ice tea.

"I tried calling you last night—about eleven."

"How come?"

"I had an idea for you—about the nightmares."

"Really?"

"Yeah. Where were you? I know you don't go to bed that early."

"You may not believe this—but somebody called just before eleven—somebody from the past."

"Not Donald?"

"Unfortunately, yes."

"Denise, you've got to stop with that guy. You know he's bad news."

"You may not believe this, Edie, but I really want to get rid of him. It's just that I can't. Whenever he shows up, it's a hard luck story, and I just can't let him—suffer."

"So you suffer instead, huh?"

"Yep."

They were both aware of a presence near their table and looked up from their conversation almost simultaneously. He stood there, food tray in hand watching them. Both Edie and Denise eyed him with obvious appreciation. Good looking, blond, maybe thirty-five. Denise could almost hear Edie salivating (but she kept it under control). Denise recognized him. No white coat this time but he was the one who had gently sent her on her way yesterday when she dared to consider exploring territory not allowed to mere mortals without security clearance.

"Do you mind if I sit here?"

Edie didn't miss a beat. "Be our guest."

He sat down and they watched as he carefully removed each item from his tray neatly, then carefully laid the napkin on his lap.

He was suddenly aware they were looking.

He smiled (a rather endearing smile, no less). "Oh—I'm Richard Kramer."

Again Edie was quick. "I'm Edie Pulaski and this is Denise Burton. We work in Hillman's office—Denise is in charge."

"Nice to meet you—both."

He started eating. He was a careful eater too. Neat, fastidious. Small portions. His mother had taught him well.

It was Denise's turn.

"You know, we met yesterday—up on the sixth floor."

A slight surprise. "Yes, I remember. You were lost. What were you doing up there anyway?"

"Just delivering some stuff."

Edie refused to be left out. "Say, what goes on up there anyway?"

"Oh, not much really. We're just doing some experimentation."

"With live animals?"

"Yes."

"Sounds pretty gross."

"Oh, I assure you we use all proper care, and they're all treated humanely."

Denise was curious. "Why all the hush-hush security stuff?"

"Oh, it's because these are military contracts. They want to keep everything strictly controlled—at least until we have some results."

He was about halfway through his meal, when someone came up behind him. The someone was tall and rather important looking—white coat and all.

"Richard, we need you upstairs."

"I'll be right there."

Edie's turn. "Say don't those guys even give you a decent lunch hour?"

"Well, we're in the middle of something. Lunch will have to wait."

"And I thought *we* had lousy jobs."

"When Papa Marikem calls, you just have to snap to. No rest for the weary scientist, you know. It's been pleasant meeting both of you."

And neatly re-assembling his tray to dispose of the refuse, he was off.

They watched him leave. Edie's imagination was already racing ahead.

"Now if a guy like that asked me out, wow, I wouldn't hesitate for a minute!"

"He's probably married."

"I didn't notice a ring—but that's no sure sign these days."

"Well, he looked pretty compulsive to me. Did you watch the way he ate?"

"Who cares. The guy's a hunk."

"That's for sure."

"You ought to go after him, Denise."

"Oh, come on. He's probably younger than I am."

"So what. If you don't, I sure will."

"Good luck."

5 ❖
Sweat and Blood

TUESDAYS SHE AND EDIE met at aerobics class to move and sweat and try to get in shape. The large room in Van Nuys was on the second floor of a shopping complex. The walls were covered with mirrors producing (she always felt) the double indignity of suffering and watching yourself suffer. They worked out—almost keeping up with the youngsters— but often fudging a bit on the number of repetitions. Denise often thought about taking a class that provided a less strenuous workout, but Edie insisted this was the best and they needed a real challenge. The instructor was good and she kept them all moving vigorously to the blasting rock music in the background.

When they finished, Denise always felt she must have lost about thirty pounds, but the scale hardly showed any change. So much for all that sweat.

Frequently after class, she'd drive a few miles west to see her Aunt Vanessa.

Visting Aunt Vanessa was something Denise both dreaded and enjoyed. She was her mother's sister—older than her mother by at least eight years, and, now that her mother was gone, her only surviving relative. For the last four years she had been in a nursing home, and, while she still had most of her faculties, getting around was a major problem for her. Fortunately the money she had put away for a "rainy day" had been well invested, and she was now able to spend her remaining years in a decent place, knowing full well what she would have had to endure if her resources had been minimal.

Vanessa Cipriotti was a woman who overwhelmed you

from the moment you encountered her. She had dark hair and eyes—the Mediterranean look one seemed to associate with Italians. And she was Italian—with a vengeance. She spoke animatedly, slicing the air with dramatic gestures. She was now many pounds overweight, but there was the vestige of a beautiful woman still there. She was sixty-four years old and had taught school for thirty-five years. She was a high school English teacher, outspoken, dramatic, loved by almost all her students, and hated by almost all her administrators. And all for the same reason: she said what she felt whenever she wanted to. The kids loved her since she never restrained her unbridled enthusiasm for what she covered in class. They flocked to sign up for her classes and reveled in her dramatic readings of Shakespeare (it was always a high point of her reading *Julius Caesar* when she proceeded to assassinate herself, fall dramatically down to the floor, then rise to deliver minutes later—as Antony—the dramatic funeral oration as the class shouted the crowd's responses).

And she told her supervisors exactly what she thought of them. Her personnel file was well over two inches thick when she retired—with evaluations and criticisms from everyone she dealt with, and her acid responses neatly and dutifully typed out in rebuttal. She would have taught forever, inspiring the students and annoying the powers that be, but her body began to give out.

She had been hit by multiple sclerosis over ten years before, and the deterioration had been gradual but inexorable. Now she could only get up and down with great effort. Fortunately the attendants at the home, Pleasant Hills, were caring and kind.

Vanessa had never married. She had had some flings with a wide variety of men, but her own outspokenness frequently got her into trouble. Men liked her but backed away when she started telling them—in graphic clarity—about their faults. She was fun on a date, but intimidating, and her male friends eventually decided that living with Vanessa would be a challenge indeed.

Denise tried to visit her a few times each month although she found the surroundings depressing. The place was kept neat and clean but all around her—as she moved along the hallways—was the evidence of the incurable illnesses, the limitations of the aged, the sad condition so many people had reached after years of health and vitality. Denise often wondered just what her own fate would be and where she would end up when she could no longer function.

But when she reached Vanessa's room all depressing thoughts seemed to vanish for a time. Vanessa was witty and wise and very direct, and she was always full of ideas and suggestions. Yet having such a brilliant woman locked into such a restricted life added to the sense of depression and when she left, Denise always came away feeling sad and helpless.

"So what's with the nightmares, huh, Denise?"

"Still there."

"I still think it's all a carry-over from that time you had your tonsils out when you were seven. I remember how terrified you were of being in the hospital. Everything scared you. I never saw such a relieved child the day they brought you home."

"It could be. I've decided to see a therapist."

"Christ, that'll be a waste of money."

"Oh, my health plan covers most of it."

"It's still a waste as far as I can see."

"Well, nothing else seems to work."

"Did you try some of the things I suggested?"

"Many times. I've changed my diet, drink warm milk before bed, even tried some of the herbal concoctions you suggested. It doesn't help."

"Hmm. Well I hope the therapist you find is better than the creeps they have me see. They all keep trying to change my mental attitude. Shit! I'd like to see them lie around here all day with all these dying people and keep a positive mental attitude! I sure as hell am glad you come by when you can. I think you're the only sane one I can talk to . Know what those therapists are? A bunch of crazies. They've been around weirdos so long it rubs off on them."

"Easy, Aunt Vanessa. You'll get your blood pressure up again."

"Look, kiddo, it's my anger that keeps me alive. If I were happy here, I'd have died years ago. And—though they don't know it—I never swallow the damn tranquilizers they bring us every day. There are enough zombies around here. I'll live my own life, thank you, not some drugged nirvana."

"Shh, Vanessa."

"Yeah, you're right. I should keep my secrets under wraps."

There was a pause and Denise handed her a small wrapped parcel.

"Don't tell me. It's gotta be a new book."

"Just some light reading. The latest Baantjer mystery."

"Thanks, honey. I still love mystery stories. Though I think I've read enough of them to guess the ending about half way through. But they're still fun."

"Bad news for me. Donald's back."

"Oh, no. That excuse for a man. What's he want from you now?"

"Food and shelter—and protection from the evil forces currently after him."

"Did you take him in? I hope not."

"Had to. The poor guy was about to be disposed of by some of his evil companions."

"Well, this may come as a shock to you. But in a way I've always liked that man. The trouble is, everything he touches turns to shit. I think he needs a real kick in the ass so he'll get his life back in order. But as long as you keep rescuing him, I don't think he'll make it."

"Vanessa, are you blaming me for Donald's stupidity?"

"I happen to remember all those stray animals you picked

up as a kid. I think at one point you had about six of them at one time. Boy, did your mother hit the roof when she found out."

"I sure remember that."

"And that's your little Donald. A nice guy who needs to learn to stand on his own two feet. Stop helping him, Denise. For his sake."

The conversation soon turned to the mundane. Denise's prospects: dim. Denise's job: pleasant but tedious.

When she left, promising to be back in a few weeks, Denise felt she had had a therapy session by an expert—good common sense from one who had never had children but who felt she was responsible for her sister's daughter—a grown woman who needed some decent advice.

The rooms she passed as she moved through the building almost reminded her of the rooms in her nightmare. But this was another variety of nightmare. How many of us would have to live it before we finished our lives, she wondered.

6 ❖
Dreams and Nightmares

SHE EXPECTED TO FIND DONALD well ensconced in her apartment when she got home. But luck was with her. He was gone. The sheets and blankets were neatly folded. There wasn't even much missing from the refrigerator—as far as she could tell. Maybe—just maybe—he was out of her life now. She hoped desperately, but in reality she doubted it. Donald was Donald and there would always be just one more time. And she never knew how soon it would be.

She made a salad and threw some leftover chicken into it. As she ate, she thought about the day—and especially Richard. Edie was right. He *was* a hunk. But she, Denise, was a thirty-seven-year old divorcee. He could have his pick of any of the sexy young things that worked all over Marikem. Why would he even show the slightest interest in her?

The phone purred.

"Hello?"

"Is this Denise—Burton?"

"Yes."

"This is Richard—Richard Kramer. We had lunch together today, remember?"

It was too much. Remember? She had been thinking about him all day. But, be careful, something told her, don't be too eager.

"Sure, sure. Uh—how are you?"

"Oh, fine. Look, I'll get to the point. I'd really like to have dinner with you sometime."

A pause.

"Dinner?"

"Yes. And not at the Marikem cafeteria."

She laughed. He did have a sense of humor.

"What do you say?"

"Sure. When?"

"How about tomorrow night?"

"Great."

"How's Chinese?"

"Chinese?"

"Chinese food."

"Oh—sure. Sure. I love it."

"Where do you live?"

"Oh, it's the old Sanderson Apartments—704 Toluca. I'm in 2B."

"Is 7:30 all right?"

"Perfect."

"See you then."

She sat with the phone in her hand until it screeched at her to hang up. This was real, wasn't it? He *had* called. They *were* going on a date tomorrow. Richard Kramer. The hunk.

She crawled into bed, fantasizing. Calm down. It's just a date. Who knows if the two of you will even hit it off together. Stop acting like a teenager. You're a mature woman (damn it). You've gone out before (not for a helluva long time). You've even been to bed with some of them (two or three, I think). And this is just a guy (yes, but it's Richard Kramer, remember?).

She drifted into a blissful sleep.

And then . . .

The mist. The endless sterile corridors. The room. Distorted figures under plastic sheets. The steady hum of the monitoring machines. And the room at the end of the ward.

Blinding light as she enters. The surgically gowned figures work methodically. Eviscerating the body. The bloody organs are removed.

Then they see her. They freeze. She can see the glistening stainless steel instruments stained with crimson in their hands. Their blood-spattered gowns. Their eyes on her.

Now they move toward her. Slowly. She backs away. They move closer. She can smell the stench of blood and viscera. Her back is to the door. She is trapped. And they move still closer.

Denise Burton awoke with a start. She sat up. Yes, she was okay. She was in her own bed. In her own room. Safe. But the dream still hung in the air. She looked at her hand. There was real blood on it! But that couldn't be. And then she realized she had scratched her rigidly clenched hand with a fingernail.

She climbed out of bed. For some reason she was more shaken this time than she'd ever been. They came too close; they were too real.

She pulled open the pantry closet. On the top shelf in back was a bottle of Cutty Sark. She poured a stiff drink into a tumbler. Her hand was shaking. It took several swallows to down it and it stung her lips and throat. But the slow warming it gave her and the numbing of her senses was what she needed. She climbed back into bed and pulled the covers over her as she curled up into a fearful, fetal position.

7 ❖
Violated

EDIE WAS DEFINITELY JEALOUS. She didn't say it and she tried to control it but Denise could tell. Even though Denise kept trying to change the subject, the news that she and Richard were going out together got Edie going. She wanted to know everything. Even though there was really nothing to tell. How did he get her number? What did he say on the phone? Had they picked a place to go? How was she going to dress? It was all boring stuff, but Denise played the game and fueled the idle conversation. She was worried about the dream, and all Edie cared about was this guy. God, what will the cross examination be like after the date? Lunch tomorrow will hardly be long enough.

Denise was tired when she headed home. The day had been nothing but constant pressure. Hillman was working them hard and a couple of nightmare-interrupted nights were taking their toll. She almost felt like calling off the date. Make it another night. But then would he call her back?

Preoccupied with her thoughts, she hardly noticed some noise behind her door as she approached it. She turned the key in the lock and moved in as she had done a thousand times before. But as soon as the door swung open, she knew something was wrong.

In the dim light she could see the chaos. The room was a mess. Overturned tables, books and papers scattered all over, drawers hanging open. And all of this registered in an instant.

In the second instant a gloved hand was across her mouth and a cold, piercing object roughly made contact with her throat. She was aware of the sharp, leather smell of the glove, then the pain as her head was pulled rudely back, and then the voice. The slow, whispered, slightly nasal voice.

"Mrs. Burton, please keep very still. The blade I'm holding against your throat is quite sharp and—well—blood stains on a white carpet are very hard to remove."

She did as he asked. Her mind flashed on the rape stories—the murder stories. Should she try to resist? He was very strong and there was that cold knife at her throat. Her very dry throat.

"Mrs. Burton, I'm really sorry about the mess I've made, but it was necessary, and I just don't have time to clean up. Now I want you to answer some questions—just nod or shake your head. Understand?"

She nodded.

"Good. Your ex-husband was here last night?"

She nodded again.

"Do you know where he is now?"

She gave the asked-for negative response.

"Do you know if he'll be back?"

Again no.

"Now this is important. Did he leave any small packages or large sums of money with you."

No.

"Think carefully now. Did he leave anything?"

Once again no.

"Your husband has something of mine and I want it. Do you understand?"

A nod. A very slow nod.

"Good. Now I want you to lie down on the floor."

Oh, God, no. Now he's going to rape me.

Her mind raced. What to do. Shall I try to break away?

"Quickly now. On your stomach."

He was twisting her arm and forcing her down. She was on her knees. Then she was forced all the way down.

She could feel his grip release her.

"Now please lie very still."

What was he going to do? Was he some kind of pervert? Was he about to attack her anally—sodomize her? Her muscles tensed.

She wanted to pray, but could not even summon up a word or phrase.

"Now please count slowly in your head to a hundred. Slowly."

His voice seemed farther away. Was he leaving? She wanted to speak but could say nothing. So she started counting. But each time she got to ten she couldn't remember any more. And she started over. Three times she started and couldn't continue. So she just lay there, sweating, listening. Her muscles were tight. She had a desperate need to urinate. But she just lay there, hearing nothing. The woolen pile began tickling her face. But the room was deathly still.

Suddenly the phone purred.

Should she answer it? She twisted her head from side to side but could see nothing in the dim light. The phone continued purring, relentlessly. Suddenly she pulled her terrified body up and reached for the receiver.

"Hello."

Again the whispered, slightly nasal voice.

"I'll be keeping in contact with you, Mrs. Burton, to see if he comes back. And you can expect me again if he does."

It was over. For now.

She collapsed into a chair. Her body was quivering. She could smell the sweat soaking her clothing. She sat for what seemed like a very long time. The shaking stopped. She was beginning to calm down.

Something told her to check the time and she could see the glow of the digital clock in the bedroom. It told her it was 6:40. And then she remembered her date.

8 ❖
Fortune Cookie

HER ADRENALINE PUMPING—the combined effect of fear, exhaustion, and anticipation—Denise was showered and changed in fifteen minutes, a real record time for her. She merely ignored the chaotic mess strewn about the apartment and flung her sweaty clothing onto the pile. Miraculously, she was even able to find a decent dress still hanging in the closet and some stockings and underthings still in a drawer. Luckily Richard was late and when the doorbell rang, she was just putting on some lipstick. On the second ring she moved to the door not quite sure how to explain the remnants of the cyclone all around her. Deciding that a first date that required convoluted explanations—including a former husband's shady dealings and a brush with a violent druggy—was not the best way to begin a relationship, she grabbed her jacket and purse and met him outside the apartment door.

"Sorry I'm late . . . "

"No problem—I was running a bit late myself."

"Aren't you going to invite me in?"

"Well, things are just a bit messy tonight."

"I don't mind."

"Maybe another time."

"Okay. Ready to go?"

"More than ready. It's been one of those days I don't even want to talk about."

"Hectic, huh?"

"Very."

"Then let's go."

It was an excellent Chinese restaurant and they feasted on a wide range of Mandarin, Szechwan, and even Hunan delicacies. Though generally not big on the spicy items, tonight Denise dug into each new taste with gusto. She ate almost as if this might be her last meal and Richard watched her with increasing delight. They talked a bit about their jobs (Richard was quite guarded), the city, their lives, and their favorite movies. It was intensive eating and, for her, frantic talking. The events of the day had made her hyper and she talked nervously, trying to forget what had happened a mere hour before. By the time they sipped their tea and the waiter appeared with the cookies, a lull had settled over their table. Denise seemed all talked out. She cracked open the cookie and read the sliver of paper. And then she started to cry.

All evening she had worked to keep this from happening, to cover for the fact that her apartment was a shambles, she had just had an intimate brush with death, and a man who could not care if she lived or died had threatened to come back and maybe kill her. But the piece of paper that lay amid the fortune cookie crumbs was just too much:

"*Some friends will bring pleasure; others pain.*"

And so she cried.

And as she sat quietly next to him in the car, she thought of what she was returning to and she cried again. By the time they reached her apartment house, she was somewhat under control and Richard, who had thus far driven quietly, decided to venture some conversation.

"It wasn't the food or the company, was it?"

"No, Richard."

"Is it your job?"

"No."

"Is there anything I can do?"

"Not really."

There was a pause and then she decided that maybe there was no more image to preserve.

"Come up to my apartment, Richard."

He followed her dutifully, still unaware of what had triggered the floodgates and not sure of exactly what kind of person he had invited out that night. And when she opened the door and flicked on the light, his confusion mounted.

"You—you really meant it when you said messy, didn't you?"

He was trying to be funny but she was already sitting in the center of the room, crying.

"Look, I'm here and I'm willing to help. Let's put the place back together and then maybe you'll tell me what the hell is going on."

So they worked together, brought some relative order out of the chaos, and gradually she told him. About her ex-husband, his phone call, his sleazy way of life, and finally, her close encounter of a decidedly evil kind.

They sat in the kitchen eating some leftover chocolate chip ice cream from her freezer.

"I think this is certainly the most unusual first date I've ever had," was his only comment.

"Me too."

"I guess you could call it comic, if it wasn't so scary."

"In a way."

"Do you really think you should stay here tonight?"

"The guy's gone. He's after Donald, not me. I'll be okay."

"Well, if you need anything, call me. Anytime."

"Thanks. For everything."

"Don't you think you should call the cops?"

"No. Not yet, anyway. There's too much explaining and it might hurt Donald even more."

"You still like him, don't you?"

"Like a puppy dog."

"A puppy dog with some vicious friends."

"Yep."

She watched his car pull away as she stood at the window

and she was alone. Alone with her problems and her night-mares.

The mists swirled again. The room came into view. The figures lay swathed in plastic. The monitors flashed. And then there was the operating room. The gowned figures. The bloody entrails.

But this time all of it seemed clearer. Images were sharper. Details stood out. The figure lying on the table was not connected to any anesthetic. She could make out a pale, lifeless face. The man was dead. Was this some kind of autopsy? And what was she doing there? Other images were clearer too. There were three gowned figures working on the body and they still had not seen her. She watched as a bloody lung was removed. wrapped and placed in a stainless steel container. Something was stencilled on the container, and she could read it:

"X-29."

And then they were watching her. Their work had stopped. They were now moving toward her—slowly, deliberately. And one held a hypodermic syringe. They moved in slow motion, but she could not turn to run or shriek. And now they were close to her and the needle was all she could focus on.

And then she was awake.

Soaked with sweat, she got out of bed, threw on a robe, moved to the kitchen, and turned the burner on under the tea kettle. She sat and sipped the orange herb tea and tried to remember the details.

9 ❖
X-29

EDIE SAT EXPECTANTLY, resisting the impulse to begin a stream of questions, as Denise walked into the office. For Denise it had been a wearing night—the intruder, the date, the nightmare.

"Before you start, Edie, let's just hold it till lunch, huh?"

"Fine with me."

But she could see Edie watching her much of the morning, as if expecting some hint or clue.

When lunch hour finally arrived, Edie led her quickly out of the office, fearful of anyone else interfering. They got their food, and Edie found a small back table and, even before Denise could have a sip of her iced tea, started in.

"Now you've got to tell me all about it. All of it. From the moment he arrived."

Denise decided that just the date would be enough—at least for now.

So she described the restaurant, much of their conversation, and the trip back to her place.

"And—"

"That was it."

"You let that hunk just go home?"

"I was tired. Edie."

"And he didn't suggest anything?"

"Nope."

"Damn. I was waiting for the good stuff."

"That's about as good as it gets."

And Denise was able to attack her salad.

It was well after four and Denise was organizing the work for the next day. She tried to make sure it was divided evenly among all the typists. As she opened a folder to check how much work was involved, it hit her.

A single phrase on the page stood out.

"Project X-29."

Carefully she examined the document. It seemed to be some sort of progress report from a department whose title and symbols (Data Research 14-AO-662) she could not remember seeing before. The term was mentioned only once and she read over the sentences several times.

"The total study will be determined by results derived from Project X-29. These results are expected by 10 March. Further decisions will depend on this data. For additional supporting data refer to files 10-B-6 and 19-B-8. Continuing analysis of subjects and their reactions will be included in forthcoming reports."

X-29.

She flipped through other pages but there was nothing. Where could she find out more? For the moment, she hadn't a clue.

10 ❖
A Death in the Family

ILONA NEAL'S FEET HURT. She had not had a chance to sit down for almost five hours and now her feet were killing her. The emergency room at Fuller Memorial Hospital had been a madhouse all morning. There were the usual auto accidents, stabbings, domestic fights, and little kids brought in for everything from skateboard falls to swallowing quarters. It had been relentless all day. When her shift ended and she headed mercifully away from the building toward the parking lot, she wondered, after many more days like this one, whether being an ER nurse was something she had perhaps done far too long. How long had she been doing it? Almost thirty years? Wasn't it about time to retire? She still liked the excitement but she didn't know how much longer her feet could take it.

As her blue Accord pulled off the freeway at Pico Boulevard and she turned south to her comfortable Cheviot Hills home, she was thinking about retirement. They didn't really need her income now. The kids were on their own. Stuart earned a handsome salary where he worked, and he certainly had not been talking about retirement—yet.

Recently, though, he had been complaining more about working at Marikem. He was becoming increasingly more critical of the company's management.

Maybe they both might think about retirement. They were only in their late fifties. It might be fun to just kick back, do some traveling, play more tennis, sleep later.

Ilona was surprised to see her husband's gray Lexus

parked in the driveway. He rarely came home before six. Was he sick?

She called out his name as she entered the house, but there was no answer. She could hear music playing in the back room office where he worked so she moved quickly through the house.

The door to his study was ajar and she called his name again, but there was still no response. As she entered she could see the green glow of the computer screen and hear the innocuous music. And then she saw the figure on the floor. The figure of Stuart Neal. Her husband.

Quickly her nurse's instinct went on automatic pilot. She crouched beside the body, felt for a pulse. But there was none. Terrified, she furiously began CPR, breathing into his mouth, putting pressure on the sternum with both hands. But it was all to no avail. The body was cold. Stuart Neal was dead.

Stunned, Ilona pulled herself up. She looked at the desk and now noticed the empty syringe that lay there. Exhausted, she collapsed into the desk chair staring at her husband's inert body. Then the tears came. She sat for many minutes staring at what had been her husband. Stuart Neal. A brilliant scientist. A marvelous husband and father. Her eyes were wet and sore. She could stare no more at what lay there. Slowly she swiveled the chair around. In front of her was the green computer monitor. And on it she read:

Ilona dearest,

This is goodbye. I'm frustrated and disgusted with my life. I can't stand my work or my day to day existence. There's really nothing to live for. I'm sorry. I love you.

Stuart

At Marikem Industries the next day Stuart Neal's suicide was talked about in subdued tones. Several of the chemists he worked with could not believe that this vibrant man had taken his own life. Others felt he had become disgruntled with Marikem and had expressed his unhappiness many times in the last few weeks. He was obviously very depressed and should have seen a therapist. For a while they talked about it, but eventually the conversation changed to the living.

Most employees of the Marikem family, however, hardly knew him. His suicide provoked just a few minutes of conversation. Then they too moved to other topics of the day.

11 ❖
Shrink

DR. KENYON GLIDDEN'S OFFICE was on the eighteenth floor of a downtown professional building. The directory was peppered with MD's and DD's and PhD's and other letter combinations far more arcane. Denise sat in the waiting room, flipping pages of *Newsweek* and not paying too much attention to the news of last month vividly presented in full color on the pages in her lap.

She felt apprehensive, but pleased she had got this far. Marikem's Human Resources Department had recommended Dr. Glidden and was even giving her time off to see him. And her health plan covered almost all of his fee. Maybe, just maybe, he could help her.

After a short wait, the receptionist, who serviced several of the doctors, beckoned for her to follow and she was ushered into Glidden's inner sanctum. He was effusive and genial, a large man, comfortably dressed—no white jacket and not even a tie. His office was hardly ostentatious: a desk, some leather chairs, a few indoor plants, nondescript prints on the walls. But no couch. She was looking around for that traditional symbol of the therapist's trade, when Glidden's deep-throated laughter boomed out.

"Yes, I do have a couch—in the next room. But most patients prefer these chairs. They really are quite comfortable."

She smiled.

"Now, Mrs. Burton, how can I help you?"

She started to talk about the nightmares, but Dr. Glidden interrupted.

"Let's have some background, first. I want to learn a bit

about you—you know, your family, your childhood. And do you mind if I record our sessions? That way I can listen to them again, and we can refer to previous sessions if we need to."

He was holding a small cassette tape in his hand.

"That's fine. Anything that might help."

"Good, good."

He opened a small drawer and clicked the tape into a recorder that she could not see. And then she began.

"I had a rather ordinary life—if you think about it. My parents were middle class. My father sold appliances, you know, TVs and refrigerators. He didn't make a lot of money. But my mother worked—as a secretary. She was the one who first taught me to type. We had enough to live on and my sister and I never thought we were poor. I guess the schools I went to—the kids all had about the same so we really didn't know much about being affluent."

"Your sister?"

"Yes, Melinda." There was a pause. "She died in a car crash about ten years ago. I was living out here. She was in Texas—San Antonio. It was a real blow. Maybe because we never had been too close and she died before we two could talk out a lot of things—"

"What things?"

"She was five years younger than I am. My parents seemed to favor me—at least I thought so. I probably picked on her—the way most older sisters generally do, I guess."

"And your parents now?"

"Both dead. My mother died of breast cancer. Even a radical mastectomy couldn't stop it. She wasn't that old either. Fifty-nine.

"My father was a smoker. We tried but never could get him to stop. He died from lung cancer a few years after my mother."

"Quite a string of tragedies."

"I guess. They all hurt for a while when they happened. I think I've worked through them."

"And your marriage?"

"That was ongoing grief. I fell for Donald too fast too soon. Maybe I was desperate. I was thirty with no immediate prospects. He was a good-looking, romantic guy. I guess I should have been wiser and tried to get to know him more before I agreed, but I was just flattered by the offer. Let's face it, nobody else had asked."

"Was he abusive?"

"Not in a physical way. I don't think he ever laid a hand on me—to hurt me. He was just—a loser. He couldn't do anything right. Jobs, friends, contacts never worked out. If it was abuse, it was a weird kind of mental abuse. He just screwed up everything—took my money. And it took me three years to finally call it quits."

"How about your sex life with Donald?"

There was an embarrassing pause.

"That was probably the only good part of the relationship. He was a tender and sensitive lover. We had good times in bed—when we had them. I think I miss that most of all."

"And now?"

"As far as sex goes, I've been pretty celibate."

"Do you miss it?"

"Hell, yeah. But I've started going with a guy now and who knows—something may come of it."

"And now we get to the reason you're here."

"Well, Donald is still one reason. He keeps popping up in my life and making things more complicated. I'm not sure which is the worse problem, Donald or the nightmares."

"Tell me about them."

"I guess you'd say that's the main reason I'm here. I have these recurrent nightmares, almost always the same. But sometimes more things happen in them, like more of the story unravelling—"

"Describe what happens in them."

And for the remainder of the fifty-minute hour Denise did just that.

The session had been a good first step, she felt. She left the office feeling drained, but with a sense of accomplishment. Maybe, just maybe he could help her work this out. Maybe she could get a decent night's sleep. Denise crossed the parking lot toward her car. It was late in the afternoon; Glidden had been able to give her an appointment because of a cancellation and she was pleased she had been able to see him so quickly.

As she turned on the ignition to her car, she was suddenly aware of another presence. She was about to turn but the voice was unmistakable.

"Denise, just drive out as you normally would. I'll stay low in the back."

"Damn it, Donald, do you still have my car keys?"

"Yep. But this was an emergency."

"Aren't they all? How did you know where to find me?"

"I made a few phone calls. Edie was helpful."

"What do you want now?"

"Look, Denise, can we go somewhere where we can talk? Somewhere private."

She pulled out of the parking lot and moved into traffic.

In a remote area of the west valley was a spot she and Donald had visited often. It was a little park tucked away at the far edge of a housing tract. Not too many people knew about it and it had gotten a bit seedy over the years. A few picnic tables, two or three barbecue pits, some trees. That was about all there was. But there were some large, dramatic rocks that formed a barrier at the far end of the park and they used to climb them when they were dating.

She parked her car in the small, deserted parking area and they walked over to the rocks. Smiling, Donald scrambled to the top and Denise followed.

"Remember this spot, Donald?"

"Sure. We used to come here a lot."

"In the bad old days."

"Well, some were good."

"Just a few, Donald. Just a very few."

"I guess you're right."

From where they sat they could see the streets below, cars frantically fighting the afternoon rush-hour traffic. The steady, slow bumper-to-bumper parade on the freeway. The noise of brakes screeching and horns blaring barely audible a mile beneath them. High up where they were, all was peaceful and serene.

"So what is it now?"

"There's a guy after me."

"I think I met him."

"Met him?"

"Yes. He broke into my apartment a few days ago and scared the shit out of me."

"What happened?"

"Oh, not much. It was the day after you were there. He made a mess of my things, stuck a knife at my throat, and made me lie down on the floor. I suppose he's not big on rape, huh?"

"No. Not that I know of. Was he a short, black-haired guy?"

"Sorry, I never saw him. But he had bad breath and a kind of whining, nasal voice."

"That's him. Vinny Haas."

"So?"

"Oh, not much. He's just out to kill me, that's all."

"And you want me to just bump him off next time I see him."

"It's not funny, Denise."

"No, it's not. You got me into this, Donald. I thought I was through with you and your shitty friends after the divorce. Well, I want out, for good, do you understand? I don't want these sleazeballs breaking into my place and then calling me at all hours."

"I'm really sorry, Denise. I never wanted you involved."

"Thanks. Now how do I get dis-involved?"

"Well, I think I've got to get out of town for a while."

"Fine. And you'll inform all those who are out to kill you that you're no longer available?"

"After a while, they'll stop looking."

"And how do I fit into your escape plan?"

"Well—I need some money."

"Naturally. How much?"

"Whatever you can spare. I'll send it back to you when I get settled."

"Sure. Look, Donald. I don't want to give you anything. But if you'll promise that this is the end—that you won't come back to haunt me again—that you and I are finished, through, kaput—I'll give you what I have. Deal?"

"It's a deal, Denise. Absolutely."

"Then meet me back here at the same time tomorrow. Around six. I'll have the cash—not much—but enough for you to get far enough out of town. From there you're on your own. Got it?"

"Thanks, Denise."

"Do you have a place to stay tonight?"

"Yeah. And I don't think your apartment is a good idea."

"I agree with that. Can I drop you anywhere?"

"Sure. I'll show you where."

They climbed down slowly. Donald was looking less haunted. A weight had been lifted from both of them. For Denise, there was the hope of relief from this albatross. Just maybe.

She dropped him off near a spacious shopping mall in Burbank. There were several condominium complexes nearby and he deliberately avoided telling her where he was staying. For her protection, he had said. Before he got out of the car, Donald leaned over and kissed her cheek. He was almost crying and it was with genuine sincerity that he thanked her again.

"I won't forget all you've done, Denise, honestly."

And he was gone.

She drove off feeling a mixture of sadness and relief. Maybe she would be through with Donald finally. In a way, she would be sad. Having somebody who depended on you was nice in a way. I guess that's why people have kids, she thought.

The phone was purring when she (carefully) entered her apartment.

"Hello."

That voice again.

"Mrs. Burton? Has your husband come to see you?"

"Uh—no." (Not a total lie.)

"Has he called you?"

"No." (That was the truth.)

"Well, I'm sure he'll be contacting you very soon. Maybe tonight. I want to know where he is. Remember, I don't want to involve you in this at all. This is between your husband and me. But if you don't level with me, I assure you that you will suffer as much as he does. Understand?"

"Yes."

"Good. You'll be hearing from me again—very soon."

The call was over.

But the phone purred still again.

"Hello."

"Denise? This is Richard."

Thank God. She was so relieved to hear his voice.

"Denise? Are you there?"

"Yes. Yes. Sorry, I just got a call from that crazy guy who broke in the other day. I'm a little shattered. Just hearing his voice scared me."

"Can I do anything?"

She really wanted to say: Yes. Yes. Come over right now. Hold me. Protect me. I need you.

But she didn't.

"No thanks, Richard. I'll be all right."

"Can we see each other again? I'd really like to."

So they made a date for Friday night.

And Denise pulled a frozen dinner from the freezer and popped it into her microwave.

12 ❖
Research

EVERYONE HAD LEFT THE OFFICE. Denise had stayed on to finish up some work she had promised Hillman and Edie had left for an early dinner appointment. It was pleasant working in the empty office with no noise and distractions. She finished the work and was about ready to leave when she had a thought.

X-29.

Could she possibly find out more about it?

She turned the computer screen on again and started playing with it. She tried accessing information using whatever words she could:

"X-29."

Nothing.

"New Projects."

Nothing.

"Special Projects."

Nothing.

She rummaged in her drawer. She had written down the department that had been mentioned in the report.

"Data Research 14-AO-662."

She tried accessing it through this title.

The screen told her that a code was needed and she had no idea what to use. Punching in X-29 didn't work. She was stuck. She turned off the screen, frustrated.

She was leaving the building as she had all the years she'd been working there when an idea hit her. Somewhere in the vast, sprawling structure that was Marikem Industries they must keep files. Not everything could be in computer memories. There must be some back-up hard copies. Just in case. And somewhere in this complex of buildings there was a room with files in it. Real files. In real file cabinets.

She looked at the directory. And there it was. File Room. Basement. B-77.

She took the elevator to the basement. It was quiet. The long, pale hallways were no different from all the other floors. But there was a strange stillness as if few people ventured here. It took some wandering but she soon found B-77. And the door was clearly marked "File Room."

She tried it but it was locked. She noticed a button. Why not? She pushed it. Somewhere inside the room a bell was ringing. She waited. And then it opened.

The man who opened the door was old, hunchbacked, and balding. He wore a faded blue suit and a tie that was stained with food spots and definitely the wrong color—even for faded blue. His hands shook as he held the doorknob. He moved slowly and with considerable annoyance. Denise, at first was somewhat taken aback. Amid the immaculate, soundproof environment of Marikem with its handsome executives and fashion model secretaries, this man was curiously out of place. Perhaps this was why he inhabited the zones of the underworld—the basement caverns of the plant, relegated to custodian of the file room.

"May I help you, Miss?"

This was said with the same annoyance he seemed to have for any task—even coming to answer the doorbell.

"Why—yes. I have to do some research for—for Mr. Hillman."

She flashed her security pass and he grunted.

"Hillman?" He pulled a clipboard from where it was hanging by the door to check the name.

"Is that Reginald Hillman in personnel?"

"No. Lawrence Hillman. In research reports and data."

"Yeah. Here he is. Come on in."

She followed the strange man into the room. It was vast,

apparently occupying much of the basement area of this wing of the building. And it consisted of virtually nothing but row upon row of filing cabinets. There seemed to be thousands of them.

She moved down the rows looking for the system of filing, eventually realizing that the alphabet seemed to be a good place to start. She found the X's and reached for the drawer but it was locked.

"Excuse me," she shouted. "Could you help me with this drawer?"

Again the strange man lumbered to her, cursing under his breath.

"Is this the only one you want opened?" with the appropriate annoyance.

"I think so."

He pulled a massive ring of keys from his pocket, and fumbling for a few seconds, finally found the one that unlocked the drawer. She was about to open it when she realized he was standing there at her elbow, watching.

"Thank you."

But he still stood there.

"Gallagher!" A voice boomed from across the room. "Damn it, Gallagher, would you come over here? I'm on aisle fourteen."

He turned and shuffled off, grumbling and quickly Denise pulled open the drawer and found a slim file folder labeled "Project X-29."

Inside the folder there were perhaps twelve or fifteen sheets of paper. She remembered seeing a copy machine as she came in and decided that the best situation at the moment (considering she had lied to get in and might not easily get back) was to copy what she had. Quickly she moved to the machine and started the duplicating, but after the third sheet, the flashing message that the machine needed paper appeared, and she vainly searched around the area for more to put in. There was none to be seen. Above her on the wall the clock showed almost six o'clock and she wondered how long they kept the area open. Then she saw the strange custodian of the place moving down the aisle near her.

"Mr. Gallagher? Could you put some paper in the machine?"

Grumbling (naturally) he moved toward her to do the job. The paper was above her on a shelf which she should have easily noticed.

Gallagher pointed to the clock.

"I've got to close at six. Can you do that tomorrow?"

Now she had an interesting problem. Should she further incur Gallagher's wrath by insisting he let her do the remaining ten pages or so or should she take a chance on trying to get back into the room tomorrow. She decided to take the coward's way out and wait—he was obviously not the type to get on the wrong side of.

"I'll put that file back for you," he grumbled. "Be sure to sign the form showing what you've copied."

He stood there while she did, so she had no choice but to put down her name, Hillman's name, and the file information.

She stuffed the pages she'd copied into her purse, and followed Gallagher to the door.

"Thanks for your help." She tried to sound pleasant and not sarcastic but it was difficult.

"Don't mention it. See you tomorrow."

And the door closed behind her.

On the almost empty parking lot she sat in her car looking at the pages she had copied. There was a good deal of technical data about materials and references to other projects. On the second page were several references to "the experiments at Frampton Flats" with more technical data. On page three—at the bottom—there was the beginning of a list of some kind: "Subject 302—observed 21Aug showed anoxia—and tissue deterioration. Subject 96—deceased 18 Aug."

And that was all she had. She had found something but what she had found was not enough. She would have to come back and get the rest.

13 ❖
A Fond Farewell

As she moved through traffic, heading home, she kept thinking about the sheets of paper on the seat beside her. What did all this mean? But, most important, why was she involved in it? Could the nightmares have some basis in reality? Was this all some crazy construction of her mind? Or was it just some weird coincidence?

She turned a corner, passing a large bank, and suddenly remembered. "Donald!"

She looked at her watch. It was already ten past six and she had promised to meet him at the park at six.

And the money.

She parked her car—illegally—and dashed to the automatic teller machine. She punched in her code and asked the robot for the maximum (which was about all she currently had in her checking account anyway. She did have about a thousand salted away in a savings account, but that was for a vacation—or a rainy day. And that was *hers*.) Soon the ten twenty dollar bills popped out, and she was back in her car heading for their rendezvous.

He was there in the growing darkness, pacing, looking, waiting.

When her car pulled into the lot, he moved behind a tree and watched as she got out. Denise smiled. If she had brought someone along, he would not have done much of a job of hiding. Good old inept Donald.

"Sorry I'm late. I got involved in something at the office, and just couldn't get away," she lied.

"I was worried about you."

"Really? About me or the money?"

"Honest, Denise. I do care about you. I was afraid—that something might have happened."

"No such luck."

"You weren't followed, were you?"

"I seriously doubt it."

"Thank God."

She reached into her purse and pulled out the ten bills, crisp and new, and handed them to him. He took them without paying much attention and stuffed them into his pocket.

"I really do appreciate this, Denise."

"Sure, I know. Aren't you going to count it?"

"Look, whatever it is, I'm grateful. And I know you're a generous person."

"I'm just two hundred bucks worth of generous. It's about all I'm worth right now."

"Thanks."

He was about to turn and move off, but she stopped him.

"Just a minute."

He turned back and watched her move up to where he stood.

"That money is not free, Donald."

"I know—I'll get it back to you—"

"That's not what I mean. I'm buying something with it. My freedom from you, Donald. I don't care what you do with it—where you go—and I don't really want to know. Just take it and get the hell out of my life. That's all I ask."

"It's a deal."

"I mean it, Donald. Because if you show up again, the next time your sleazy friend calls me, I'm gonna take him right to you. Understand?"

"Sure, Denise. I promise this is absolutely the last time you'll hear from me. Thanks again."

He leaned over and kissed her on the cheek, then quickly moved off into the darkness.

Denise Burton stood for many minutes after Donald left. She didn't know if she should laugh or cry. Donald was gone from her life. Maybe now she could move on. Just maybe.

14 ❖
Accident

THE CAR LAY ON ITS SIDE, a battered wreck, glass scattered all over the highway. Stunned and in shock, the driver sat by the side of the road, unable to comprehend what exactly was happening. Through his dazed eyes he could see his young passenger on the gurney being stowed roughly into the ambulance. He was aware of the traffic, once halted, now starting to move as a highway patrolman gestured angrily to the gawking motorists and tried to get things functioning again.

The paramedic was now standing beside him, asking him questions, trying to ascertain if there were any injuries. But all the driver could think of was: why in hell wouldn't she put the belt on?

Rogers Kennison had just pulled his old Toyota off the road behind the crumpled wreck, and accompanied by Gerry Gotschalk, his favorite photographer, was approaching the dazed driver. He really hated this. He was embarrassed trying to get information from people too dazed or shattered by some traumatic event to want to talk to the press. But his editors thought it made good human interest, so he did it. Then he would talk to the highway patrolmen who had been first on the scene, and get their stories. And he would be sure to include if those in the car had worn their belts. And Gerry would get the photos. And the story would appear tomorrow on page twenty-two—unless, of course, something more important required the space. And then it probably wouldn't appear at all.

They drove back to the offices of the *News-Telegram* in silence. To Gerry it was just another assignment. Fires, shootings, accidents. He shot the photos they wanted and turned them in. But to Rogers it was something more. He wanted some decent reporting jobs. Things he could dig into.

Rogers Kennison was red-haired, full of energy and eager to prove himself. He was just thirty and had been an outstanding student. He was a bit chunky, already developing middle-aged spread from lack of exercise and erratic eating habits. He had come though journalism school at UCLA with dreams of greatness. The magic words had been investigative journalism. Woodward and Bernstein were still the heroes to young journalism students, even though Watergate and "Deep Throat" had long left the front pages, and many people no longer even remembered these two except maybe in their movie personifications by Redford and Hoffman.

But Kennison had read *All the President's Men.* And for him it had been a revelation. A reporter could do more than just report the news; he could help make the news. As a student reporter he dug into everything he could find. He unearthed misuse of university funds by department heads and wrote about it. He wrote a scathing article when student tuition was raised just as he discovered that some of the top administrators were getting salary increases. He was unrelenting and the student body—at least those who read his articles—loved them.

But when he graduated, he discovered a much different world. Newspapers wanted fledgling reporters to do the mundane leg work that brought no glory. They had to keep their advertisers happy.

There was not much opportunity for exposés and investigations.

He got a job as a cub reporter for the *News-Telegram* and played their game, expecting things to improve. But they never did. After several years reporting the fires, accidents, and local political news, he was tired of it and was seriously considering looking for another job. Maybe somewhere out there was a newspaper that wanted something that might rock the boat. Maybe.

They were jammed in freeway traffic on their way back to the office and Rogers decided to speak his mind.

"Gerry, I'm thinking of leaving the paper. Maybe try to get something somewhere else."

"Like what?"

"Another reporting job where they won't just assign me to a shit beat day after day."

"Do you really think other papers are any better?"

"Who knows? It's worth a try."

"Sure. That's easy for you to say. You're not married and can bounce around all you want. I'm sticking where I have some security. It ain't much but it is a living. And I get paid for takin' pictures. That's fine with me."

"But I want something more, Gerry. Something more challenging."

"Fine. But make sure you have somethin' in hand before you take off. It's a tight economy out there and a lot of papers are goin' under. And there are a hell of a lot of bright young kids comin' out of journalism school who'll work for a lot less than you will. Don't jump into things too quick."

Gerry was known for his pragmatism. He was a gangling six-foot black man with an incredible amount of horse sense. He had a flashing smile and winning way with everyone he encountered. He looked like a basketball player, but all through school, in spite of playing a little, he had been more attracted to photography. In high school he had latched onto the photo instructor and spent every available moment shooting pictures or working in the darkroom. He got a part time job in a photo shop and learned all he could there. He spent two years in junior college, but felt he knew enough and started looking for jobs. On the basis of his portfolio (which included some award-winning pictures) he was hired by the *News-Telegram*, and now he did what they wanted him to do, and he had fun. It wasn't art, but it was what he liked and they paid him for it.

Rogers always could depend on him for good counsel. And he knew Gerry had been talking good sense. But he was itching for something that would challenge him, and maybe it was time to start looking for something that might provide that challenge.

They were off the freeway now, in the downtown traffic. In a few minutes they would be back at the old building that housed the *News-Telegram*. Rogers would dutifully file his story and dream of greater journalistic challenges. Dreaming was about all he could do right now.

15 ❖
Friday

DENISE WORKED BUSILY DIRECTING the office. Her pace was almost frantic. It was Friday and it would be an important Friday for her. Donald was gone. She had bought her freedom for 200 pieces of silver. When she finished her work, she would head back to the file room and perhaps find out more about Project X-29. And then there was the date. Richard would be picking her up at 7:00. There was a lot to do today.

She finished her work promptly at 5:00—expecting Hillman to come out of his office any minute with something for her to do that would keep her after hours. But he didn't.

She gathered up her things and was about to leave. Edie was watching her with interest.

"You're sure in a big hurry today."

"Yeah. I've got lots to do."

"Big date tonight?"

"No—well, yes actually. But I've got to get some other odds and ends done before I go home."

"With Richard?"

"The date? Yep."

"How's that developing?"

"Oh, I don't know. It's only the second time we've gone out, Edie. We both believe in doing things slowly. We hardly know anything about each other."

She had gotten up to leave.

"Well, keep me informed." There was a sly humor in this reaction. The implication was: I'd love to know but you probably won't tell me.

"Sure, Edie. See you Monday."

And Edie watched her go.

But once out of the office, Denise headed for the basement. She took the stairway down—avoiding the elevator and trying to make sure no one noticed her.

Things were quiet—evidently many employees had left early for the weekend and she got to the door of the file room without anyone passing her in the hall.

She rang the bell and, after a minute or two, the misshapen form of Gallagher opened it.

"Yes?"

"I was here yesterday—for Mr. Hillman. I need to finish copying that material I was working on."

"Yeah, I remember you. Couldn't find the copy paper, huh? Well, c'mon in."

He followed her as she moved back to the aisle of files where she had found the material on the previous day.

"This is the one I need."

Again the strange man fumbled with his enormous key ring until he found the appropriate key and unlocked the cabinet.

"Let me know when you're finished. And there's plenty of paper in the copy machine today." He chuckled and moved off.

Again Denise opened the file cabinet. But something was wrong. The file she had found yesterday on Project X-29 was gone. Feverishly she went through the folders in the drawer. Had it been mis-filed?

But it was not there. She had missed her chance yesterday. Someone had taken the file she needed and there was little she could do now about it.

She shut the metal drawer with a loud, annoyed clang and moved toward the door.

As she reached the end of the aisle and turned, suddenly there was Gallagher standing in front of her. He eyed her slowly.

"What's the matter. No copying today?"

"No. I—I don't need to."

"Too bad. I filled the machine just for you."

Denise looked at this strange man. He stood in her way. Was he blocking the doorway? What kind of a weird confrontation was about to happen here?

"You haven't been here before, have you?"

"No. Just yesterday."

"Well, you should come more often. I can help you if you need something. That's my job."

He was staring at her. He ran his tongue over his lips as he stood there. But he did not move.

Suddenly the bell rang. Another customer.

Gallagher turned and moved awkwardly to the door. Denise followed at a respectful distance, and, as he opened the door, quickly moved out as two men moved in. As she moved out into the hallway, she turned and could see Gallagher watching her and smiling with an almost evil smile as the door slowly closed.

Back at her apartment, she now was able to take her time preparing for her date with Richard. This was a lot different from the frantic pace of the last one.

She showered a long, leisurely, almost sensuous shower, feeling guilty for wasting all that water, but enjoying the self-indulgence as the hot stream caressed her body. She chose each article of clothing—underwear, stockings, blouse, skirt—with infinite care, selecting and rejecting until she had the combination she felt looked perfect.

She sat at her tiny makeup table for almost a full hour doing her face—a subtle makeup that accentuated her eyes, added a touch of color to her cheeks, and brightened her pale lips.

When the doorbell rang, she was ready, and she moved quickly to answer it. As she reached to open it, she hesitated. Since confronting her unwanted visitor before the last date, she had gotten more cautious. She had almost forgotten that caution just now.

She used the peephole, assured herself it really was Richard, then opened the door.

"You look spectacular."

It was an honest reaction from him and it reassured her that what she had done was not too much. She had done all the right things and he noticed. He, too, looked great. It was his casual look; he put on ties for his business attire. To go out he felt more comfortable with open shirts—well chosen—and casual slacks. So he wore a gray checkered shirt, navy blue trousers, and a white linen jacket. Together they looked an impressive couple.

He drove to a small Italian restaurant on a side street in Sherman Oaks—off the beaten path. It was a Friday night but the place was only moderately busy and they were quickly ushered to a small table with a bright checkered tablecloth and a flickering candle. Soft music played in the background and the waiter seemed to know Richard—he obviously was a frequent patron. They had drinks and shared a marvelous antipasto.

Then came steaming minestrone. Denise felt she was already well taken care of, as far as food was concerned. But the waiter soon arrived with the main course—cannelloni. It was superb.

Richard insisted they share a small bottle of Chianti, and soon, the wicker-covered bottle shared space on the table with the other delicacies as they ate and drank in the romantic surroundings.

By the time the spumoni arrived to complement the evening, Denise was stuffed, happy, and slightly tipsy.

As they were sipping their coffee—Denise chose decaf—Richard suggested a late movie. Denise, feeling warm and mellow by virtue of the wine and the delicious food, agreed, and soon they were back in the car heading for a small art theater on Ventura Boulevard.

They had arrived a few minutes late, and Denise missed the title, but soon she settled in to watch the subtitled French film. It was a murder mystery, very compelling, but also highly sensual.

Not long into the movie the detective was undressing a beautiful blonde suspect and the two of them were soon coupling in the bedroom of her lavish apartment.

In a later scene the two of them—high on marijuana—did a quickie in the kitchen, the woman thrust up against the counter. Still later another couple was discovered in bed by the detective as he burst in to question a suspected killer.

There were at least two more very erotic scenes and Denise kept thinking the film was pretty close to being out and out pornographic.

It was, however, all done with exquisite style in the photography, the lighting and music. And, of course, there was a plot that transcended the thinly developed stories of the traditional porno. It was engrossing—but it was also highly arousing.

As the lights came on after the credits ended, Richard and Denise sat staring at the now blank screen. The remaining customers moved up the aisle and in a few minutes they were the only two left in the theater.

"Interesting choice of movie," was her only comment.

"It was about the only thing still playing this late—and it had been recommended to me by several people. What did you think?"

"Hmm. Pretty erotic."

"Did you think so? Considering a lot of films these days, it was pretty tame."

"Really? I must have been missing some really good ones, I guess."

"What a shame. I'll have to show you one some day soon."

She stared at him in the dim light. He was a good looking man. In the subtle lighting he looked somewhat mysterious—

like a character in a movie like the one they'd just seen. To her he was still much of an enigma, and the lighting suited him. She tipped her head back and closed her eyes and in a moment she could feel his face close to hers and his lips kissing hers. It was a surprise—but a very pleasant surprise and she responded by returning the kiss.

It was a long and emotional one, and when he moved back and she opened her eyes, she could see him staring at her.

"That was nice," she said.

And without being asked, he moved to her again and they repeated it, now with arms around each other and they held it for a very long moment.

A voice behind them brought them back to reality.

"Sorry folks, have to close up."

They broke their embrace, and, somewhat embarrassed, moved up the aisle and out of the theater.

They drove home in silence. She was thinking how pleasurable those kisses had been and how much time had gone by since a man had really kissed her like that. Would he do it again? Where was this night leading for both of them?

He parked half a block down from her apartment.

"Would you like to come up—I have some liqueur—a friend gave it to me. It's very good."

"Sure. A good way to end the evening."

Did he mean that? Or was there more on his mind? She wasn't sure.

They sat in her kitchen, sipping the liqueur. She had put a CD on—some Mozart— and the mood was romantic.

"You know, Richard, you've hardly told me anything about yourself. I always feel that me and my problems tend to dominate our conversations."

"Oh, there isn't much exciting about my life. I worked my way through school—got my Ph.D. in biology—now I work for Marikem."

"Your family?"

"I'm an only child. My parents divorced when I was about ten. I don't see too much of either of them. My father lives on the east coast, my mother up north—in the Bay Area."

"And what exactly do you do at Marikem?"

"Basically, whatever they tell me. We do a lot of work—experimentation—for the military. Most of it is security stuff and I'm not supposed to talk about it."

"Experimentation?"

"Yes." He seemed uncomfortable and rose.

"It's been a nice evening but I think I should be going."

She got up also.

"Yes. I enjoyed it."

She followed him as he walked toward the door.

"Can we see each other again?" she said, as he reached for the doorknob. It was as if something had suddenly gone wrong, but she couldn't figure out exactly what.

He turned to her abruptly.

"Denise—"

But instead of completing the sentence, he pulled her to him and kissed her again—and again. They were hungry, sensual kisses, and she didn't resist. She responded, kissing him in return, giving herself up to him, letting him kiss her eyes and her neck—and then he lowered his head to kiss the nipples of her breasts through the silk of the blouse. Her mind flashed to the images of the film. Here in the ordinary surroundings of her drab apartment, it was as if the film was being repeated, but now it was for real, and it excited her more than anything she had experienced in many months.

He had unbuttoned her blouse, being careful not to be violent with the buttons or the material. He was a careful man. Now he was kissing her breasts, his tongue licking the nipples.

"Richard—Richard."

He paused and looked up at her, and she pulled away from his ardor and extended her hand. He took it and—almost formally—she escorted him to the bedroom. In the dim light she stood by the bed and slid the skirt off and the panties and stood opposite him wearing only the blouse that hung almost to her knees. He undressed quickly; she watched as he dropped, neatly on a chair, his shirt and pants and stood wearing only his distended jockey shorts. He slid off his shoes with quick motions and moved to her. Again they kissed passionately and she could feel his erection pressed hard against her. His hand slid down between her legs. He began to caress her and soon to run his fingers deep within her. She was amazingly moist and kissed him on his neck and chest.

Again she pulled away, but this time moved to the bed and he followed.

Soon they lay facing each other. She embraced his midsection and ran one of her hands down into the undershorts, massaging his erection and then with both hands pulling the shorts down. He rolled over on top of her, his hand stroking her clitoris, and was about to enter her, but she pulled back.

"Don't you have a—"

"No—I may have one in the car."

She rolled over and with one hand opened the drawer of the night table and took out the tiny wrapped parcel.

He was about to reach for it but she held it away from him, tore it open, and removed the rolled condom. She slid down to face his erect member and carefully unrolled it, fitting it to him and continuing to massage the erection as she did. Then she rolled back onto her back and opened her legs to receive him. He slid in easily and soon they both moved to a similar rhythm.

It was over a bit too soon for her, but it was good and she hugged him and they rolled over to the side still tightly together and kissed long and lovingly.

And then the phone purred.

Almost unconsciously she picked it up from the nightstand and heard the too familiar voice.

"Mrs. Burton—is he with you now?"

"Who—"

"Your husband."

"No."

"I know someone is there. I can hear him."

"It's not Donald. I don't know where he is."

"Don't lie to me."

"I'm not lying. Look, I told you it wasn't Donald. Now stop harassing me."

The caller clicked off.

They lay there side by side quietly. The evening had been spoiled for her. And once again Donald had been responsible.

"I shouldn't have answered."

"It's okay. Forget about it. At least he waited till we finished."

She laughed. "The thoughtful hood."

She turned to him and kissed him gently on the mouth.

"This has been wonderful, Richard."

"And we'll do it again sometime—very soon?"

"I'd like that."

She watched him as he rose from the bed. He was well built and moved gracefully. She watched his silhouette as it moved to the bathroom. She heard the flush and the water run in the sink and he reappeared and pulled on his clothes. Then he moved to her in the bed. He leaned over and kissed her and then he was gone.

16 ❖
Excursion

THE SUNLIGHT COMING THROUGH the slits in the venetian blinds hit her in the face and she blinked, then rolled over. It was about seven but she didn't care. She felt luxurious. It was Saturday, and she had all day to revel in what had happened last night. Richard had made love to her. She felt delicious—sensually alive again. How long had it been? She did not want to think about it. It had happened and it was good, and it might well happen again. She ran her hand down between her thighs and touched herself. It felt good—almost like re-living the events of the night before. She enjoyed the feeling and continued massaging, stroking her clitoris, running her fingers inside herself. She had not done this for a long time either and the experience felt warm and sensual. She contin-ued the movement, thinking about the night before, Richard's hands touching and commanding her, and after many minutes, the orgasm came. She shuddered with the de-light of it and rolled over breathing hard. She lay there think-ing about all she had been missing—but last night had been better and she looked forward to seeing him again, yearning to have him inside her.

She stayed a long time in the shower, letting the hot water cascade all over her, again feeling guilty about wasting the water yet wanting to continue this feeling of sensuality—wanting to hold on to the sensation of her body—her woman's body—her body that a man now desired.

Even the smell of the morning coffee was an almost sex-ual sensation and she sipped it slowly, letting the aroma rise up her nostrils and the hot liquid trickle down and warm her whole body.

As she reveled in all these sensations, she suddenly realized there had been no nightmares. Her sleep had been untroubled and she had had a restful night. Was this the secret? Did she need a night of lovemaking to take away the onus of the nightmares?

If this was the antidote, she would gladly accept it. All she needed was someone to supply the medicine on a regular basis. It was a remedy she would have gladly paid any doctor to prescribe.

At the corner of the kitchen table lay the papers she had copied from the file on Project X-29. Once again she looked at the information but there was not enough—not enough to understand what all this was about. Except—

The reference to Frampton Flats.

Frampton Flats.

Somewhere she had heard that name. Was it in a newspaper article or on a TV program?

She pulled open one of the drawers that regularly collected various junk she couldn't bring herself to throw away and found an old road map. She spread it out on the table and searched for the location. Somewhere was a place called Frampton Flats. And then she found it. A tiny spot in the desert. Not even a town. Not listed in the directory. Just an afterthought. But it was there and it did exist.

It looked as though it was about an hour or so driving distance based on the map and she realized her day was free. Why not? Take a little excursion into the desert. See the spring flowers. Maybe even get some clue about what was out there. In Frampton Flats.

Denise packed a few items in the car: a thermos of water, some food, a jacket and an old baseball cap that had been Donald's. She grabbed the roadmap, and headed out for parts unknown.

The day was lovely and she was a bit sorry she hadn't

thought of asking Richard to come with her. But this was really her own thing and she had to work this out for herself. Who else would believe her? Who else would pursue this quest to understand a nightmare?

The sequence of events was almost unreal, but Frampton Flats was there. It had been mentioned in the file material, and she had found that from the image in the dream that showed her Project X-29. Was she on to something or was this all some bizarre series of coincidences that her own subconscious was creating? Maybe she would find out.

She headed out on the freeway leaving the city behind her and was soon in the suburbs where homes were fewer and the landscape was dotted with an occasional shopping mall. Soon she found the highway she wanted and exited the freeway heading north. And then the vegetation grew more sparse and the desert began to appear. It was a bit too early for many wildflowers, but an occasional patch of poppies or lupine or yarrow would appear here and there beside the road.

About an hour had passed and she was losing the radio station that provided the mellow music that had kept her company so far. There wasn't much out here and she looked vainly for some road sign or indication of where she was.

Then she saw what she was looking for. A sign indicating the road to Frampton Flats. It was weatherworn and about to fall down but it pointed to the left where there was a narrow asphalt road almost imperceptible since sand had covered it through years of minimal use. She turned and headed where the sign pointed.

The sign indicated that Frampton Flats was three miles, but it was a slow three miles since the road was bumpy and full of potholes and broken asphalt. After twenty minutes of gut-jarring bumps, Denise could see something up ahead. A small cluster of structures. As she approached she could see no sign of life. It was a ghost town. But it was hardly a vestige of pioneering days. The structures were modern. Some nicely built houses, a street of shops. But not a soul in sight. At what had probably been the center of town she stopped her car and got out. A breeze was blowing and the dust and tumbleweed provided the only movement in this strange, empty setting.

It was something she had never experienced. Walking along a totally empty street, looking at buildings that once had had people in them but now were vacant and quiet and desolate. Judging from the peeling paint and broken windows and the piles of sand against the sides of the structures, it had been a long time since someone had lived here. Where had they all gone? What had happened?

For a moment she felt lightheaded. Alone in a desolate town here in the middle of nowhere. What did this remind her of? Then it came to her: "The Twilight Zone"! Wasn't there an episode like this? She racked her brain trying to recall the show but it had been too many years since she watched the old black and white re-run and what did it matter? This wasn't television created from Rod Serling's vivid imagination. This was reality. And Denise Burton was standing alone in an empty town in the middle of the desert.

Slowly she walked the main street. The signs indicated a drug store—Reeves' Pharmacy (24 hr service); a hardware store—People's Hardware (Equipment for rent—Tools Sharpened); and a small market—Wong's Market (open 6AM to 12 Midnight). She approached each one and looked through the windows, now mostly boarded over. Inside she could see empty shelves and dust-covered displays. Spider webs hung everywhere and occasionally a rat scampered in the dust.

Further down the street was a small gas station and convenience store. Except for two old wrecks that had once been pickup trucks there was nothing here either. The two hulks of metal sat rusting, tires gone, windows broken, another symbol of this abandoned community.

Beyond the center of town neat stucco houses spread out on small side streets. But here too there was no sign of life—

no cars, no people. Scrubby desert vegetation had been left to grow at its own pace and now it even poked its way through cracks in the cement pavement.

Denise had an urge to move closer to these houses—to look for the signs of those who had at one time inhabited this now forgotten town, to ferret out more of this enigma begun with a dream.

The first house she approached was small and had once **been** pink. But the desert sun had washed out most of the **color** of the stucco and the wood trim was cracked and peeling. At the door she was tempted—as a civil person— to ring the bell, but the idea seemed rather ridiculous. The door was not locked and she pushed it open to inspect the domestic desolation more closely.

She expected the house to be totally empty, but it wasn't. There was some furniture— encrusted with grit—even an occasional picture on the wall. Where the storekeepers had had a chance to pack up and move their merchandise, the homeowners must have left more abruptly or taken only their necessities. Most of the drawers hung open, empty of contents, and cupboard doors stood ajar.

She walked to another house and found an almost similar situation. A few broken chairs, an old kitchen table, a stuffed living room sofa that had seen better days. In the closet she opened there were a few items of clothing: a faded pair of jeans, some children's blouses, but mostly it was just dust, and rats, and spider webs.

As she left the second house and walked back to her car, she was aware of an almost imperceptible presence. For some inexplicable reason Denise felt she was not alone here. She could see no one but she had the feeling she was being watched. Someone else was present, but where? Maybe the emptiness was getting to her and she was experiencing some kind of paranoia. She reached her car and looked around suddenly. But there was still no one in sight.

Slowly she drove the few streets of Frampton Flats. The

narrow roads all came to abrupt cul-de-sacs. Except one. So she followed this road as it meandered away from the town. For a few minutes she saw nothing but empty lots, then there was a fork. Denise chose the right fork and continued for another few minutes. As she came over a rise, she could see a huge barbed wire fence—perhaps ten feet high and stretching for miles in both directions. She reached the spot where the road ended as it came to the fence. There was a gate, but a heavy chain with a padlock clearly gave evidence the road stopped here. And there was a weather-beaten metal sign:

Frampton Flats Test Facility
Marikem Industries
This Facility Closed Indefinitely
Restricted Area
Positively No Trespassing

So Marikem was here. Beyond that fence there was something—a "test facility." Whatever that meant. But the sign and the locked gate were formidable preventive measures. Just what the installer had wanted. Keep out. Stay away. Go home. This means you.

Denise drove back and tried the other road. She thought of the famous Robert Frost poem. Frost, she thought, would have been jealous. She remembered memorizing the poem for school. He had had to choose one road. She was able to try *both*. After a few minutes the road turned sharply to the left and then moved steadily downhill.

Suddenly she was confronted with a small grassy area—quite different from the desert terrain. A fence surrounded it but this fence was low and decorative and not formidable at all. Then she realized what lay before her. It was the town cemetery.

Strange, a tiny hamlet that she estimated had housed maybe two hundred people, with its own cemetery. She counted the small markers. There were over fifty graves. All carefully maintained. What a strange contrast, she thought. A deserted town with a neat cemetery. Someone still kept this graveyard watered, weeded and neat.

And that was all. She had seen just about all there was of Frampton Flats. The quick tour. All, of course, except the "test facility." Perhaps next time.

Denise drove back trying to make some sense of it all, but there were still too many confusing elements, too many loose ends. She realized suddenly she was very hungry. and pulled over at a roadside rest to eat her sandwiches and sip some water. Then she headed back to the city.

17 ❖
The Man of Her Dreams

THERE WERE FOUR MESSAGES on her answering machine. Richard. A short, friendly "how are you doing" type message (just like him) that certainly belied their last night's intimacy. Then Edie inquiring about going out for a movie or shopping on the weekend. Then *that* voice. The voice that reminded her that he was still waiting for Donald—still watching her apartment. God, she thought, I certainly hope Donald is about a zillion miles away by now, and this guy will give up looking for him (fat chance!). And then there was Richard again, sounding a bit worried about her, wondering where she'd been all day, wanting to get together again. Wow! That was worth it all, she thought.

Denise called Edie back and suggested maybe some Sunday mall shopping—but she wanted to keep the evening free. And when she called Richard back, she got his machine. She said she was happy to hear from him and would love to go out again. She did not return the call to Donald's "buddy." She really must get his phone number next time he called. Sure.

By five there was no call from Richard and she guessed he had gone off somewhere, but decided not to call him again. Two messages might look a bit too desperate. She thought about calling Edie but figured shopping with her for half of Sunday would be about all anyone could stand. So she called her favorite pizza place, went out and picked up the pepperoni delight and stopped by the local video store to see if anything current was there. No luck. It was Saturday and all the new releases were checked out. So she settled on an oldie

(Redford and Streisand in *The Way We Were*) and headed home for her evening of solitary entertainment.

It was almost midnight when Denise headed for bed. She was tired but felt good and quickly lapsed into a deep sleep.

And then the images began. Blurred at first, then coming into sharper focus. Again the hallway. Rushing down the long corridor and entering the ward where the figures lie draped in plastic. The beeps and clicks of the monitoring devices. The door at the end of the room.

Moving to it, slowly, hesitantly. Then the operating room. Watching the gowned figures surround the body. Even more focused now, she can see the bloody entrails as they are removed, examined, measured, put into cannisters. This time she clearly sees each body part. Heart. Kidneys. Lungs. The snake-like intestines. The stomach. Then the sudden freeze-frame as they see her. The gowned figures, stopping, watching the interloper, moving toward her. As one comes closer, she can see the syringe, its needle long and glistening, in his hand, and she can hear the echoing voices. The figure is closer now and Denise cringes, frozen in fear. But this time she sees past the masked figure who advances to her. Behind him the others also move to her. And one is removing his mask. And the image of the face is sharp and clear. It is the face of Richard. Richard Kramer. Her Richard.

18 ❖
Shopping and Dining

WHEN DENISE AWOKE, she felt shaken, vividly recalling the details of the dream. Quickly she jotted down what she remembered. Dr. Glidden had suggested this, but she rarely had to write them down. It was all too vivid and the details of the scenario were made sharper by each repetition. But what was Richard doing there?

Were the events of the dream now getting mixed up with her real life? What did all this mean?

She met Edie for shopping and lunch, and while Denise bought very little in the hours they spent at the mall, she felt better getting away from her problems and this bizarre sequence of events that seemed to keep unfolding.

At lunch Edie wanted to know about how her relationship with Richard was developing. Denise was non-committal but did say he had called a few times and they would probably go out again. Edie was involved with a new boyfriend but he worked nights so they weren't seeing each other as much as she wanted. They had finished lunch and were sipping the decafs when Denise finally said, "The nightmares are happening again."

"The same ones?"

"Yes. Same weird ones. Same weird story."

"Have you told the shrink?"

"Yeah. So far he hasn't said much."

"When do you see him again?"

"Tuesday—after work."

"Push him a little. Maybe he can give you a pill or something. Some of them even do hypnosis."

"I'll ask him."

They were silent for a moment then Denise said what was really bothering her.

"In the dream last night, Richard was one of the guys in the operating room."

"Richard?"

"Yes. Richard Kramer."

"So?"

"Well, it's strange he should be in it, isn't it?"

"I dunno. Lots of times I have dreams where my sister pops up. I even had a weird one a month or so ago and Hillman was in it."

"Hillman?"

"Our boss. And this is funny. He was running after me. And he was stark naked. (She giggled) And boy does he look silly with nothing on!"

"I can imagine."

"So don't worry about seeing Richard. I'm sure he's gonna pop up a lot now—especially if you keep seeing him."

"I guess you may be right, Edie. I never thought of it that way."

The phone was purring as she entered her apartment, and it was Richard.

His voice was animated and playful, "Hey, stranger, you're a hard person to reach."

"You're not so easy yourself, Richard. I *did* call you yesterday."

"Oh, yeah. Thanks. They called me back to Marikem Saturday. There was some problem I had to help them work out. No big deal though."

"Are you ever free of that place?"

"No. Not as long as we're involved in this current research. It should be over soon, though."

A pause.

Then Richard, casually, "Say, how about a date?"

"When?"

"How about right now? I could pick you up for dinner—and it doesn't have to be a late evening since we both work tomorrow."

"Well, okay, if you promise—"

"Scout's honor."

"Okay."

"I'll be there at 6:30. Okay?"

"Fine. I'll be ready."

Denise showered and changed and, true to his promise, Richard was there at 6:30. He took her to a small cafe on Ventura Boulevard. It looked very exclusive. There was hardly any indication on the front door—just a tiny sign in the window and the lights inside were dim. Soft chamber music could be heard in the background and the tuxedoed waiter ushered them to a small side table. And when Denise saw the prices, she was a bit taken aback.

"Really getting lavish, aren't we, Richard?"

"Oh. The prices? Well, this place is worth it. As a matter of fact, I'm going full tilt. We'll order some top notch wine from the wine list."

And he showed off his prowess by picking a delicate rosé (expensive too) that marvelously complemented their seafood.

It was a festive meal and Denise forgot all about the prices and reveled in the food, the wine, and Richard's company. They talked animatedly (the rosé helped) and as she watched him—glancing occasionally at the good-looking man opposite her—she felt lucky to be going out with a charming guy who took her to places like this and treated her with such kindness and generosity. And as she remembered their lovemaking, a warm glow came over her. Was this a relationship that could go somewhere? Could she and Richard someday make a permanent commitment? Relax. The wine's getting to you. You're trying to skip ahead to the last chapter. No fair.

He took her home. The meal had lasted almost two hours and it was close to nine o'clock. They sat in the car and he put his arm around her. It was a marvelous, long, passionate kiss.

"Would you like me to come up?"

She hesitated. He was kind. They both wanted to, but he was leaving it up to her.

"Well—"

"Your choice—unless you want to leave it up to me."

"If I did?"

"I'd say definitely yes."

There was only a nightlight on in the apartment—that and the lights from the street, and as she shut the door behind them, there was just illumination enough to provide the kind of atmosphere they both wanted. They kissed again as they stood in the living room. A long, sensual kiss. The wine and the food made her feel warm and comfortable, and she returned the kiss eagerly.

In the bedroom he undressed her, slowly, running his fingers over her skin, neck, shoulders, breasts. He knelt and kissed the nipples, running his tongue gently over them. She was excited and could feel his excitement as, still kneeling, he pulled her skirt down to the floor, and kissed her midsection, running his tongue over the navel.

Then he slowly drew the panties down over her hips and thighs and knees till they lay at her feet on the floor. She stepped out of them and stood in the dim light reveling in his sensual gentleness, and she quivered noticeably as he kissed her thighs and ran his tongue across the mound of hair, moving up and down with a gentle, lapping movement.

It was too much. She shivered and pulled away, moving to the bed and sitting on the edge. She watched him pull off his shirt and trousers, leaving them in a heap on he floor. His own excitement—for once—transcended his customary neatness. Then he kicked off shoes and pulled off socks (which took an awkward few seconds) and stood looking at her figure as she sat at the bedside. They were both shadows in the glow from the windows but she could see him as he lowered the jockey shorts, revealing the dramatic erection; she could feel herself eagerly melting in the sensual moment.

He sat next to her and she reached out to touch him between his legs, gently stroking him and watching his face as he tipped it back in obvious pleasure. He turned her face to him and kissed her lips, her cheeks, her eyes, her neck, and as he ran the tongue down to her breasts, his hand slid between her legs, stroking, caressing, then entering her and continuing the slow methodical motion.

She fell back on the bed enjoying the sensual rhythm as he rolled over her, mouth on breasts, fingers moving in and out, then fondling her clitoris as he continued the motion. Her eyes were closed but she heard him fumble in the drawer for the condom and the sound as he tore it open.

Then he was in her, sliding in, beginning to move. She responded, moving her hips in sync with his, uttering small whimpering animal cries as his breath came heavier and the pace of the rhythm increased. And then she could hear a moan coming from his throat. A moan that continued as he moved faster and faster.

Then it was over. But he kept moving, now slowing the rhythm, slowing, still slower. He rolled their two bodies together to the side.

He kissed her again on the lips. A long open-mouthed kiss and she could feel his stiffness diminishing yet she kept pressed to him, her hips pushing hard as if she never wanted him to leave—never wanted the moment to be over.

They were sleeping now, a sheet thrown casually over their naked bodies, pressed side by side. It was a glorious sleep, the culmination of the meal, the wine, the lovemaking. Richard snored gently, his breaths long, his chest heaving. Denise slept peacefully, still, her breathing almost imperceptible.

It was almost three when he awoke and moved to the

bathroom. Then he started, awkwardly, to pull on his clothing, strewn across the bedroom floor. He had a bit of trouble locating one sock in the darkness and as he crawled on the floor, looking for it, Denise awoke.

"Richard?"

"Yes, it's me."

"What is it?"

"Just looking for my sock."

He found it and pulled it on, sitting on the floor. Her eyes finally could make out his clothed figure in the darkness.

"Are you leaving?"

"Yep. It's after three. I've got to get home."

He was all dressed now and moved to the bed where her naked figure lay, covered only by a sheet, her breasts making a prominent outline. He knelt by her and kissed her, his lips warm and soft.

"Thanks," she said simply.

He laughed gently. "Thank you!"

As he moved to the door, she rose and stood in the darkness, remembering the warmth of his lips and his body, remembering the magnificent evening they had spent. Richard and Denise. Denise and Richard.

19 ❖
Sweat and Worry

THE MUSIC POUNDED in the backgound as Denise and Edie worked away following the instructor's lead, moving legs and hips and arms and legs and hips and arms and legs and hips and arms. The workout was almost over and Denise looked at the clock on the wall. She felt totally worn and doubted she could make it to the end. But she did.

They sat in the locker room, too numb to even move. Finally they pulled off their soaking workout clothes and moved to the showers. Denise wondered if it ever got any easier. For her, every week seemed harder. She really had to take an easier class. She wasn't twenty-five anymore. That was for sure.

Later they sat at the juice bar sipping a concoction that was guaranteed to be non-fattening and was supposed to be good for you.

Denise certainly hoped so.

Edie seemed less worn than she was. She had started her incessant litany of comments on everything: the people they worked with, the people in the aerobics class, their jobs.

"Did you see that article in the paper yesterday?"

Denise hadn't.

"About all the companies involved in military work?"

"No, Edie. I haven't even looked at a paper in days."

"Jesus, Denise. They're all cutting back. Aerospace people are being fired by the thousands. The big electronics companies are getting rid of people left and right. And most of the lay-offs are right here in good old Southern California."

"Have there been any cutbacks at Marikem?"

"Not yet. But you know we're up to our ears in military work. It can't last."

"So what do we do?"

"I don't know. My new boyfriend suggested I do some looking around. Even consider leaving the L.A. area."

"Look, Edie, I'm sure we could get something else if we had to. Good word processors can work anywhere."

"Sure. Good word processors are probably a dime a dozen."

"Well, maybe you're right. But the people in charge at Marikem seem to know what they're doing. They've been around a long time and I'm sure they want to survive."

"Maybe. But I'm not gonna stay if somethin' else comes along."

"Fine. But there's been a lot of talk about converting to peacetime stuff. You watch. I bet Marikem is working on doing that right now."

"I hope so. I hate goin' out to look for a job these days."

"Me too."

"You ought to ask your new boyfriend. He seems to know what's happening at the plant. He would know if things are lookin' bad."

"Good idea. I'll see what Richard says. Ready to go?"

"Yep. Enough exercise for one day, huh?"

"More than enough."

And they headed out to their cars.

20
Head Trip

IT WAS HER SECOND VISIT and Denise had lots of questions she wanted to ask. She had told the doctor about her parents and sister and a bit about her growing up. Then there had been a long explanation of the dreams in as much detail as she could remember and Doctor Glidden had listened attentively, nodded a great deal, and made a few perfunctory remarks. She had told him about her evolving relationship with Richard. She wanted to hear more from him, but so far had gotten little if anything. Maybe it just took a while for the relationship to warm up. (Longer than her relationship with Richard had taken.) At the end of the first session she made a mental note to jot down some questions. Maybe it was her turn to start asking—to find out more about what she had come here for in the first place.

"So how are you, Miss Burton?"

"Okay, more or less."

"Good. Good. And the nightmares?"

"Not so many since I last saw you."

"That's good news. Any changes in the scenario?"

"A few."

"Like?"

"Oh, some details are sharper and there was one strange thing in the last one—"

"Yes?"

"I told you about Richard—"

"Your—friend."

"Yes. Well, he turned up in the last dream. Strangely too."

"Strangely?"

"He was one of the doctors in the operating room."

"You recognized him?"

"Yes. He had his mask off for a moment and I definitely recognized him."

"Hmm."

"Do you think that has any significance?"

"Probably not. He is somewhat important in your life now, right?"

"Yes."

"Well, it's not uncommon for real life people to appear in dreams—fathers, mothers, lovers—even teachers and superiors."

"But it was so weird. When I saw him there."

"Of course. The subconscious works in many strange ways. It unearths experiences and mixes them up in line with our fears and anxieties. Some analysts feel that many images are sexual in nature."

"Sexual?"

"Yes. May I ask if your relationship with Richard is—well sexual?"

"Well—yes—it's become that."

"Has it been pleasurable?"

"Yes. Very much so."

"Do you want to talk about it?"

"Well—we've been to bed together twice. He's a very gentle lover—and quite sensitive to my needs."

And with a bit of prompting, she described in more detail their two lovemaking episodes. Dr. Glidden said little during her explanation and she wondered if he was titillated by the erotic details. Denise felt embarrassed at first but after a few minutes (with little response from the doctor) she relaxed and described what had gone on. As she talked, she felt the whole thing seemed rather cold, describing what had been (for her) moments of intense pleasure in a rather clinical way. But she presented the narrative dispassionately like a health teacher talking about sex to a high school class. It certainly took the fun out of it all, she thought.

By the end of the session she had almost forgotten about the list of questions she had prepared, but as she rose to go, Denise suddenly remembered and took out her list.

"I know it's late, but could you answer a few questions for me?"

"I'll try."

"Why am I having the nightmares?"

"I'm not sure yet. I may have some answers soon, though."

"Why is it always the same—with things getting added each time?"

"Serial dreams are quite common. What you're experiencing happens to many people. Maybe not the same way or with the same exact scenario but our literature has ample evidence of this sort of recurring dream experience."

"And is there any way to stop it? It's starting to wear the hell out of me."

"Perhaps. There's no medication, but hypnosis sometimes works. And we may try that soon. I just need to find out a bit more about you. More clues to get to the bottom of all this. Understand?"

"I think so. Thanks. I won't keep you any longer. Thanks, Dr. Glidden."

"No problem, Miss Burton. See you next time."

In the waiting room, Denise suddenly remembered a question she had neglected to ask, so she quickly re-opened the office door. Dr. Glidden sat at his desk, a small audio cassette in his hand, and he was just about to drop it into a large manila envelope. He looked up as she entered.

"Yes—Miss Burton?"

"Oh—I had just one more question—"

"Could you perhaps save it until our next meeting? I have another appointment waiting and I'm running just a bit late."

"Oh, okay. No problem."

As she turned to go, she saw that something official seemed to be stamped on the manila envelope. She wasn't sure, but it looked like "Private" or "Secret" or something important like that. And Dr. Glidden seemed rather sheepish, his professional demeanor gone for the moment—almost like a little boy caught in the act of some youthful indiscretion, smoking or playing with himself in public.

And as she moved through the waiting room, she was surprised to note that it was totally empty.

21 ❖
Two Visitors

SHE HEADED HOME. Maybe we're getting somewhere, she thought. But why was he so uncomfortable when I came back in? I guess he can't deal with being caught without his professional face on. Hypnosis. That's something I've never done before. Might be an interesting experience.

It was almost seven when she got home. She pulled a frozen dinner from the freezer and put it into the oven. Not one of her favorites.

She put on some music, a Mozart symphony her Aunt Vanessa had given her. She turned up the volume. Though the apartment walls were rather thin, everybody on her floor seemed to play their TVs loud so she did the same. She suspected that most of her aging neighbors were hard of hearing. She made a cup of instant coffee, and sat down in the kitchen to wait for the dinner to be ready.

There was a knock at the door.

Strange. She wasn't expecting anyone. Unless one of the neighbors wanted to borrow something. Mrs. Bolofsky down the hall always seemed to run out of decaf and old Mr. Maloney downstairs always had something he wanted to talk about. She suspected Maloney was a dirty old man at heart and probably wanted to walk in on her sometime when she was in her underwear or headed for the shower. Poor guy. His timing was always off.

Denise had learned to be cautious since her episode with Donald's "friend" so she put on the door chain before she opened it. Through the opening she saw a pathetic sight.

Donald. Again. Her ex. Her nemesis. Her albatross. Donald. Forgotten (almost) but not gone.

"Quick, Denise, open up, will you!"

And though she probably should have slammed it in his face, she did what he asked and let the wreck called Donald Burton back into her life.

Again he looked like the man she had picked up on skid row just weeks ago. Dirty. Disheveled. At least two days' growth of beard. He would have fit in with the refuse that haunted the inner city. The druggies. The two dollar hookers. The hopeless.

Perhaps some were genuinely down on their luck. Victims of society. But others had destroyed their own lives through drink, drugs, despair. And where did Donald fit in?

The remains of Donald Burton moved into the kitchen, dropping exhausted into a chair, his head collapsing into his folded arms on the table. He was silent for some minutes and Denise was not sure just what to say. Then he looked up at her across the table.

"I'm sorry, Denise. I know you've heard that from me before. But I truly am sorry. I didn't leave town. I was afraid they'd be watching for me. I spent the money you gave me and I'm back to square one. On the run. Scared. Nobody to turn to."

It was the same story. There just seemed to be no end to it. Donald. Her perpetual cross to bear. Back again.

He was tired too. Even too tired to eat. Though she offered him a frozen dinner (hers was ready), he said no. She ate and he watched, his eyes glossing over, his hands shaking. She thought of Frost's poem, "The Death of the Hired Man." It was one of her favorites. And here was Donald, like the hired man in the poem. But he had not come home to die (she hoped not). He had come home because she would take him in. She would always take him in.

And then, before either of them could respond, it happened.

When Donald had come in, she had taken the chain off the door. But had she locked it? In an instant it was kicked violently open and whether or not it had been locked before became an insignificant issue.

Denise knew in an instant who the intruder was though she had never seen him before. If one wanted a single word description of the man, it would definitely be "greasy." The black leather jacket, the gloves (she remembered the smell of those gloves over her face), the slicked down long black hair tied back in a pony tail, the lean wiry build, the scarred face. This was the man who had visited her before. He looked just like the way she would have pictured him.

Donald snapped awake, his eyes fearful as the intruder strode into the room. They both noticed the revolver in his hand—small, black, and shiny.

"Vinny!"

He spoke slowly, the voice matching the rest of his persona, but Denise unmistakably remembered it.

"It's been a while, Donald, and I've been looking for you."

"I've been away, Vinny, or I would have called you."

"I'm sure you would have." The sarcasm oozed.

"I've had a tough time."

"It sure looks that way."

Vinny had moved to the table and he sat slowly down eyeing them both.

"Mrs. Burton. Nice to meet you—face to face."

She did not reply. At this moment she hardly knew where she stood in the scheme of things. Whether to be sociable, annoyed, or sarcastic was not a guessing game you play when you face a man with a gun—a man probably with no compunction about using it.

"Donald, you and I have to settle some business. There's a little matter of twelve thousand dollars."

Donald had never mentioned the amount of his debt, and

when she heard the words, it shook her. No wonder the intruder was so dead serious about it.

"Look, Vinny, I don't have it. If I did, I would have given it to you. Honest—"

"And the coke?"

"It's gone. I was ripped off by your own buddy—Leonard—Leonard Worcheck. He's got the stuff."

"But that's not my problem now, Donald. It's yours. You were the one responsible, and—one way or another—you're the one who's got to make good."

Denise watched the two of them. She was witnessing a cat and mouse game, with very high stakes. Donald was fully awake now. A lot was in the balance. Perhaps his very life. And, come to think of it, maybe hers too. But Vinny sat quietly, confident of his superior position. He casually laid the gun on the table in front of him as if it was his pile of chips in this high stakes poker game.

"Now we're going to explore some options, Donald. We're going to figure out just how we can straighten out this rather substantial debt of yours."

Denise was watching Donald—a man who had come into her apartment just minutes ago: hang-dog, beaten, exhausted. Yet now his eyes flashed and his body began to come to life. Suddenly almost before she was aware of it, he leapt from his chair across the table.

He wanted the gun but his sudden movement had tipped the table over and the gun—as well as her TV dinner—now were knocked somewhere on the floor. Donald had landed on top of Vinny whose chair had gone over backward and the two of them were now struggling on the kitchen floor.

But Vinny had the edge and Denise watched as he rolled over on top of her ex-husband and his hand—in a rapid motion—pulled a switchblade from his pocket and snapped the blade open.

Donald fought to keep the weapon away and it slashed

his hand as he grabbed the wrist of the man hovering over him.

Then she saw it. The black, shiny object that had skidded across her vinyl floor and now lay just a few feet from her. The gun.

Donald's voice was a cry for help: "No—Vinny—no—"

She had the gun in her hand—and now she remembered the sessions on the firing range. She could see the two men struggling on the floor and in just minutes Donald would be the loser. She knew she had to act. Methodically she released the safety catch on the weapon. Carefully she aimed and pulled the trigger.

The blast was shattering as it fired and recoiled in her hand. And four feet in front of her she watched the back of the head of a man she barely knew splatter like a smashed grapefruit with bits of blood and brain splashing on her refrigerator door.

There was an arrested moment as Vinny paused in the struggle unaware that parts of his head were now imbedded across the room, painting a bizarre picture on the white door; and then as if suddenly realizing what had happened, the body of the late Vinny Haas slumped heavily to the floor. The blood continued to ooze. Donald lay stunned—as stunned to be alive as Denise was stunned as she stood—hot gun in hand—perpetrator of the final act in the drama of a drug dealer.

22 ❖
A Night in the Desert

DONALD WAS DRIVING. The car was speeding along the highway, heading out of town. She had let him drive though she didn't even trust him to do this, but Denise was so rattled that she was afraid she would be unable to get them anywhere. The events of the evening had been shattering, and her whole body was shaking.

Nobody in the building had reacted to the shot. She suspected those who could hear it must have thought it was from some violent TV show. But first they had the body to deal with. Then the mess.

Luckily Denise had a large trunk that she had inherited from her parents. They had moved it from the garage, and, with a bit of tugging, they had forced the corpse into it and been able to (barely) shut the lid. There had been a lot of blood and bits of skull and brains to be located all over the room. But she had let Donald attend to that. The emotional shock had finally gotten to her and, after the body was forced into the trunk, she collapsed on a chair as the realization hit her that she had just killed someone. One squeeze of a trigger had extinguished a human life. True, he might have been a scummy, drug dealing low-life. At least this was on Donald's say so. But he was dead now and she was responsible. She was in shock as she sat on the kitchen chair, staring at the trunk while Donald washed and mopped up the room.

Later as they dragged the temporary coffin down the stairs, Mrs. Bolofsky had stuck her head out of her door wondering what was happening. Denise assured her she was not moving out, just helping Donald move some things of his.

Fortunately no one else noticed them move the massive burden down to the car, and, with TV sets blaring throughout the apartment house, her rather deaf neighbors remained oblivious.

Now the trunk was jammed on the seat behind them and each bump in the road produced a rattle of the corpse within it. In the trunk of her car she had remembered to put some spades the manager kept in the garage and a small pick. She also took a large flashlight she kept in the apartment that she had bought after reading about earthquake preparedness in a magazine. She had yet to assemble all the other items suggested in the event of a disaster. But now she had a disaster of her own to deal with.

Denise opened her eyes and noticed the speedometer.

"Christ, Donald, slow down. You're doing eighty-five."

"I just want to get rid of this thing as soon as possible."

"Sure. And if we get stopped for speeding and the cop takes a look in the trunk, that may slow things down just a bit, huh?"

"They need probable cause to search the car."

"How about the blood stain on the outside?"

"That might do it."

He quickly let up on the accelerator and the car slowed to seventy.

"Try about sixty-five, please."

"Okay." He touched the brake pedal and they slowed.

"Say, Denise, are you sure you know where we're going?"

"Yeah. We're heading toward a little deserted town I visited a few days ago. It's a perfect place to bury an unwanted corpse."

The car sped through the night. The air was cool and she rolled down her window to enjoy the blast of wind.

Once they left the freeway she watched carefully for the turnoff—a bit more difficult to pick out at night—but she recognized the landmarks, and was able to get Donald to slow enough to make the turn to Frampton Flats. They drove for a few minutes, then she noticed a grove of Joshua trees and suggested Donald pull off the road. It was dark but the moon gave enough light for them to see where they were going and he pulled up among the strange shapes of the trees and stopped where she suggested.

They took out the pick and spades from the trunk and Donald carried them to a small clearing.

And then they began the back-breaking task of digging in the sand—which was at least soft on top—to create a fitting resting place for Vinny Haas—a resting place they hoped no one would discover for many, many years. So they dug. And dug. And dug. And each time Donald wanted to stop, Denise (the practical one) insisted they go deeper. And wider. And longer. She wanted to be sure the trunk would fit, not just the body. She wanted every bit of evidence deep in this hole in the desert.

When she finally felt it was big enough, they were both exhausted, and slumped down next to the grave, dirty, tired, and sore. Denise realized the trunk was still in the car, and at that moment, she didn't think she had enough energy even to contemplate dragging it out. But Donald moved to it, and was able to get the massive coffin out by himself, and she helped him drag it across the sand.

In the eerie darkness, they looked at each other. It all seemed like a scene from some macabre horror film. Disposing of the evidence of their crime. For one brief moment Denise had pangs of conscience.

"Donald, we never even thought about calling the cops. This guy broke into my place. It was self-defense. Nobody would convict me of murder. He was a sleaze. We rid the planet of him. We'd probably get a medal from the mayor."

"Sure. But Vinny has friends. Not many but enough to come after us. And a medal from the mayor doesn't help much when some druggies are out to get you. Believe me, I know."

"I guess you're right. Hey shouldn't we get rid of any ID he has? Just in case he's found some day."

"Probably a good idea. I'll do it."

Denise held the flashlight, as Donald unlatched the coffin of Vinny Haas.

Then he opened the trunk and fumbled through the dead man's pockets, pulling out some change, some plastic bags of pills, and a wallet and keys. Denise noticed the keys.

"Oh, shit, we forgot about his car."

"Don't worry. I know what he drives. I'll take care of it in the morning. I know a good place where I can ditch it, too."

Donald opened the wallet. There was a substantial wad of cash in it. He counted over five hundred dollars.

"Not bad. Crime does pay, huh?"

"Ours or his?"

"Good question. I'll split it with you."

"No thanks, Donald. I can't get excited about blood money. It's all yours. And you need it more than I do," she lied.

"Well, at least take the two hundred I borrowed."

Reluctantly she agreed and suggested he hang onto it until they were back at her place.

Suddenly they both heard the sound. It was a car coming down the road from Frampton Flats. They both froze.

"Quick," Donald whispered, "get down."

They crouched behind a Joshua tree as the headlights moved by them, apparently oblivious of their presence, and the car headed toward the highway

"I thought you said this place was deserted."

"I thought it was. But I guess somebody still goes to Frampton Flats. I just wonder who."

"Let's get this over with, Denise. I don't want somebody coming along and catching us."

So they dragged the trunk to the grave and let it slide in. As it fell to the bottom of the hole, Donald suddenly directed his flashlight beam on a corner of the trunk. There was a tag hanging on the box and he jumped down into the hole to remove it.

"Jesus, Denise. I don't think you want to leave your name and address attached to that trunk. Good thing I saw it."

Awkwardly he climbed out as she extended her hand to help.

Then they shoveled the sand back and spread the leftover sand all around. Donald took his spade and tried to smooth out the area to disguise the marks the dragged trunk had made. Denise swept the flashlight beam around to see if they had left anything, and, content that all looked reasonably okay, they climbed back into the car and Donald moved behind the wheel. They took off down the bumpy road.

"Do you think we can really get away with this, Donald?"

"Maybe. I don't think anyone will really care too much about Vinny. He comes and goes a lot so nobody really keeps tabs on him. And he lives alone. Probably the only ones who'll get curious are the dopers he supplies, and pretty soon somebody else'll move into his territory."

"You said he had friends."

"A few. But a missing Vinny won't make much impression—for a while. Not the way a dead Vinny would."

"Maybe he owes some guys money. They'll be looking for him."

"Maybe. But there are more that owe money to him. And I don't think they'll lose a lot of sleep if he doesn't show up to collect."

"You mean people like you?"

"Not quite. I'm sure most of the debts aren't quite as big."

"That's a hell of a lot of money you lost."

"Yeah. And now I guess the debt's settled. Thanks to you, Denise."

"Right. I always manage to get you out of the scrapes you get into, don't I, Donald?"

"One way or another, huh?"

"Yeah. One way or another."

As the car turned onto the highway, she tipped her head back, closed her eyes, and thought about the grisly events of that evening.

Then, exhausted, she fell into a restless sleep.

23 ❖
Lover

SHE DOZED WHILE DONALD DROVE. She was unaware of the time as the images flashed by. The images of the bizarre events of the last few days. But the one image that kept repeating was of the dead body of Vinny Haas, lying on her kitchen floor, the debris from his head scattered around the room, and she, standing, gun in hand, responsible for the death of someone she barely knew.

She slept fitfully. Images began to merge. Burying the body in the desert sand. The strange deserted structures of Frampton Flats.

And again Vinny's bloody corpse. But then came the bodies in the room in her recurring dream. And the surgery. Then a blurry face moving toward her. Then the face hovering above her, Richard's face. But not loving. Cold. Clinical. Vicious.

As the face hovered above her, she could feel the force of others holding her down. Struggling was of no use. Then came a sharp pain in her arm. The pain of a needle. Instantaneous and sharp. And then nothing. A void. Blackness.

Someone was shaking her. Rudely.

She awoke to see Donald. Donald sitting beside her. They were in the car, but they were stopped.

"Denise. We're back."

"Oh, Donald. I've had the craziest dreams."

"You've been muttering all the way home. Weird stuff. I couldn't make any sense of it."

"That's what it was— a bunch of crazy stuff."

They walked slowly to her apartment.

"Do you mind if I sleep here tonight—on the sofa?"

"It's okay. I feel a little safer now that our friend is no longer after you."

"Me too."

They were inside now and he turned to her.

"Denise, you saved my life tonight. I've got a lot to thank you for, but tonight you really did it for me."

"It was just instinct, Donald."

"Whatever it was, it was great—and I love you for it."

He took her in his arms and held her.

It was a warm and loving embrace. As he held her, she remembered the love that had once been there between the two of them and how good it had been for those years.

Suddenly he kissed her tenderly on the mouth and the feelings returned. She felt a longing for him as they stood there—a deep longing for this man who—she had hoped might be gone from her life—but was now standing here holding her and kissing her.

She knew he wanted her. And in a way she wanted him. She thought for a moment of pushing him away. Their relationship was over, wasn't it? Richard was the new man in her life.

But he was kissing her face and her neck and arousing all those old memories as her body responded to the sensuousness he knew she felt.

Now she was returning the kisses and she knew he was aroused as he pressed against her and massaged her breasts and ran his hand down between her legs.

She gave herself to him, forgetting everything—Richard, the dead body, the agony that was Donald—thinking only of how good he made her feel.

Soon their sweaty, dirty clothes lay scattered on the floor and the two naked bodies rolled on the bed in the darkness. The memories of their past lovemaking returned as she felt his body slide down and his mouth encounter her thighs, then the overwhelming ecstasy of his tongue licking her labia, driving her into a paroxysm of delicious excitement. And then when she felt she was about to explode, he was in her, moving slowly, then increasing the tempo—until they both screamed out as it happened. But he did not stop his motion and she lay and luxuriated as he kept it up and made her moan and sigh, moan and sigh for many minutes.

Soon they were asleep. Just a sheet covered their naked bodies as they lay embracing, exhausted from the long night of violence and death and love.

The buzzer on her alarm was sounding; she had almost forgotten that it was a work day. Denise clicked it off and noticed that Donald had scarcely noticed the sound at all. He lay snoring, oblivious to the fact that some people still had to work for a living. Denise looked at him, then slid the sheet off and admired his naked body. He was showing signs of middle age spread at the midsection, but overall he still looked much like the man she had married those many years ago. She replaced the sheet and moved off to the shower to begin her morning's routine. Was there a chance she could resume a life with Donald Burton? Hardly. He was a good lover still. But as a human being there seemed little chance he could ever make it again.

After all, marriages don't survive on sex alone, do they?

But she could ponder all this another time. She had to get to work.

24 ❖
Head of the Class

THE AGING LECTURE HALL was filled. The ten tiers of desks that rose from the stage to the top of the classroom were jammed with first year students, writing notes with a feverish intensity, lapping up each word of the man who stood beneath them on the raised platform. The room was old and had seen many thousands of young faces over the years. The tables and chairs were well worn and the ceiling revealed cracked paint, but few noticed these minor details.

Almost all of the two hundred eager faces sat entranced by the performance of Dr. Marcus Kominsky. He was well along in years and heavyset, but he moved animatedly at the front of the lecture hall, gesturing, filling the board with formulas, posturing, and putting on a magnificent show.

Even though he was teaching a freshman chemistry section, Kominsky put all the fervor into the lecture that others might provide to some advanced seminar. He had been teaching at Cal Tech for over thirty years and was acknowledged as an expert in his chosen field, but he still insisted on teaching beginning chemistry each session. He felt sincerely that getting young people interested from the beginning was a primary responsibilty of good teachers, and thus each year he chose to instruct two sections of general chem and one of advanced. The students flocked to sign up for his classes and they were always well worth it.

Kominsky's techniques were fascinating. He never stayed with the nuts and bolts of his subject. He was constantly off on tangents, involving history, sociological trends, current politics, and personalities in the news. For him chemistry provided a jumping-off place to talk about virtually everything in the world. And yet, miraculously, he always covered the prescribed material. Most important of all, Kominsky's students learned their chemistry.

At this moment he was finishing a lecture on the halogens—with particular emphasis on chlorine. He had managed to cover its use in World War I as a poison gas and rambled on to the subject of poison gasses in general, their use throughout modern warfare, and the ethical implications.

When he had finished and dismissed the class, a host of fervent young future scientists crowded around him assaulting him with questions and challenging his views. It took him a full half hour to satisfy the eager students—who would have stayed much longer if Kominsky hadn't pleaded hunger and his need to have lunch. He promised them he would pursue some of the issues in a future lecture.

Marcus Kominsky was seventy-two years old. He had resisted all efforts to get him to retire and fought tooth and nail with the administration to keep working. Even though it took a special vote of the academic senate and board of trustees, and agreement by the university president, he got his way. Kominsky was an institution and he intended to keep on teaching until he collapsed—and probably then he'd do it from a wheelchair if he could still talk.

Now as he moved at a sprightly gait across the campus, an observer who didn't know him (and there were indeed few of those) might assume he was years younger.

He unlocked his cluttered office, dropped his bulging briefcase on the floor, and checked the voice mail. He hated the phone system they now had, preferring the old way of picking up messages from the operator, but the elaborate new communications system was instituted as a cost cutting measure and he had to live with it.

There was just one message. A voice from the past that he remembered well. He dialed the number and his name immediately got him through to the caller, Heinz Leiber, head of research at Marikem Industries.

"Marcus! Great to hear from you. Thanks for returning my call so quickly."

"No problem, Heinz. Oh, I heard about Stuart Neal."

"Yes, that was tragic, wasn't it."

"Was he depressed?"

"Some said so. I didn't really know him that well. He was a very private man."

"Yes, he always was."

"Did you get to the funeral?"

"No. I don't like funerals. They remind me too much of my own mortality. But that's not why you called me. What's on your mind, Heinz?"

"Just your style, Marcus. Get right to the nitty-gritty, huh?"

"You know me well enough, Heinz. We can save the small talk for another time."

"Then I'll get right to it. How would you like to come over and work here—just for a few days a week."

Marcus Kominsky took a long breath.

"I have a job, Heinz. And it happens to be a job I like."

"But what about retirement? You've been doing the same thing for years, Marcus. What about a new challenge?"

"Don't you remember? I tried a new challenge over at Marikem back in the seventies. You know how I felt about it then."

"But things have changed now, Marcus. We're involved in a major changeover to civilian activity. Military work is dead. We need people like you to come up with new ideas for the future."

"That's funny, isn't it. You have to contact a seventy-two year old fart like me to develop new ideas. What about all the young ones you've hired over the years? Are they too full of the Marikem bullshit to think on their own?"

"Now, now, Marcus. It's not the age of the scientist that

counts. You've always been light years ahead of your time and I'm sure you still are. Why not just come over here some afternoon and meet some of the people we have now? It's been a long time and you might discover things have changed a lot."

"And is Mathison still head man?"

"Of course. It's his company. But you may find him a different person from what you remember."

"I have trouble believing that, Heinz. I can't believe Meredith Mathison is any less unscrupulous than he ever was."

"Well, you may change your opinion. It's a new climate now. Come over and see. How about next week? Have lunch with me. I'll give you the grand tour."

"I'll think about it, Heinz. And I'll call you back."

"Great, Marcus. I'll look forward to hearing from you."

Marcus Kominsky sat for a long time after he hung up. He had vowed never to work for Marikem again. And Leiber had just conned him into a possible acceptance. He was about to pick up the phone, call him back, and tell him where to stick the job. But he stopped. Maybe he should take a look. Maybe things had changed somewhat. Maybe.

But now he was hungry. He got up and headed for the faculty dining room. He wondered what the lunch special was today.

25 ❖
Return

DENISE SAT AT THE CAFETERIA table with Edie. It was Thursday and she was glad the week was ending. What a week it had been. The strangest thing of all was that here she sat, calmly eating her lunch and chatting about inanities, and just a few days ago she had shot a man to death. And she had buried the body in the desert. Did she feel any remorse? Hardly. He was gone and out of her life—let's hope forever.

And Donald. When she came back from work, he was gone too. He didn't return that night, and he left no information about where he was or if he intended to return at all. A strange man. A great lover but a strange man.

"So Donald's gone again, huh?"

Edie had almost picked up her thoughts—that is, all except the details of the dead drug dealer which she was keeping totally to herself.

"Yep. No message. No word. Gone."

"Keep your fingers crossed. Maybe this is finally it with him."

But did she really want him gone? That was the strange part. She really didn't know.

"Could be."

"What about Richard?"

"I haven't seen him—or even talked to him in days."

"Well, you may have a chance this afternoon."

"Why?"

"He happens to be coming this way as we speak."

And there he was. Moving across the room toward their table. A big broad smile on his face.

"May I?" was his courteous question as he pulled out the plastic chair.

Edie's response was first. " Absolutely—at least as far as I'm concerned."

"And you, Miss Burton?"

"Well, since you're already here, what can I do?"

He smiled again. "Okay, I'll accept that."

"So where have you been?" Denise was serious now.

"I'm sorry. This place has got me working day and night. All week I've been here to the wee hours, gone home and crashed, and dragged myself back in the morning. It's been honestly hellish."

"How come?"

"Oh, it's complicated. I'll try to explain when we finish. But the worst part is they need me to go away for a few days on this project. That's what I wanted to tell you."

"Where to?"

"Oh—not far, but we'll be there till sometime next week so I just wanted to make sure you don't forget me in the meantime."

Edie again was the assertive one. "I really doubt that."

He took Denise's hand, squeezed it affectionately, looked deeply into her eyes, smiled, and was gone.

"Looks to me like the men in your life keep vanishing."

"Just my luck."

"Well, I'm sure Richard will be back."

"That's what he said."

When she got home, Donald was there. She wasn't too surprised but with Donald you never knew what to expect.

"How did you get in?"

"Oh, I found your extra key in the kitchen. And I figured I might have to come back sometime or other."

"So where have you been these last two days?"

"Taking care of some business. Getting rid of Vinny's car.

Spreading some stories around that he had left town. Trying to cover our tracks."

"*Our* tracks?"

"Okay, *my* tracks."

"And did you succeed?"

"I hope so. Otherwise—who knows what can happen?"

"Thanks, Donald, I needed that reassurance."

"Don't worry. Nothing's gonna happen. It's over and he's gone. And you and I are the only ones who know about it."

"So what are your plans these days?"

"I really don't know. I was thinking about actually getting a job."

"Now wait a minute. This can't be the Donald Burton I know. Are you sure you're not someone else?"

"Really, Denise, I've screwed up a lot of things in my life and maybe there's a chance I can straighten some of them out again."

"Like?"

"Like my life. And maybe even the thing we had going together. It could happen again."

She was on her feet.

"Now wait a minute. We had a good time in bed the other night—"

"We always did."

"Okay. But that was all we had, Donald. Everything else was shitty. And I don't have any way of knowing it won't be just as shitty all over again."

"Couldn't we try?"

"No, Donald. I can't do that again. Absolutely not."

There was a pause. She could see he was hurting. She knew that look on his face.

"Is there somebody else you're seeing?"

"What gave you that idea?"

"Oh, I talked to Edie."

"And what did she tell you?"

"Enough."

"Look, Donald. It's a relationship that's just started, understand? He's a nice guy—works at Marikem. But I just don't want to screw it up."

"Have you been to bed with him?"

"That's none of your goddamned business!"

She was angry now and he had to back off.

"I'm sorry. It *isn't* any of my business. I shouldn't have asked."

"You're damned right. Now stay out of this, Donald."

"Okay—okay. I didn't mean to make you mad, Denise. I guess I'd better be going."

"Do you have a place to stay?" Her anger had cooled quickly.

"Yeah. For a few days anyway."

"Well—the sofa's available if you need it."

"Thanks, Denise." He was at the door.

"Donald—"

"What?"

"I want you to do me a favor. You owe me."

"Sure."

"Meet me on Saturday. Here. I want to go back to the desert. There's some exploring I want to do, and I want you to come with me."

"How come?"

"I'll explain on Saturday."

"What time?"

"Oh, ten should be early enough."

"Okay."

"Do you need a ride to where you're going?"

"No. It's not far."

"See you Saturday."

"Right."

The door closed behind him.

She had every intention of going back to Frampton Flats and doing some more exploration—the town, the people in the cemetery, and—if she could, the Marikem facility that was out there somewhere. Maybe there were some answers out there. And since Richard was gone, why not bring Donald? He might prove an asset of sorts. He sure did owe her one—or two or three or many more.

26 ❖
Steve and Rogers

IT HAD BEEN A LOUSY DAY for Steve Meza. His agent had promised great things with the two interviews he'd sent him on that day, but both had been disasters. The people who interviewed him for the bank commercial had been pleasant enough, but it was clear—as he looked at the single page script—that he was not the type they were looking for. He felt annoyance as he was called to do his thing for the video camera taping the actors auditioning for the role. It was the annoyance of the minority actor who was called purely for tokenism—purely to balance the politically correct audition sheet. He knew he would never be called back.

The other interview was for a low budget film that was obviously to be made on a shoestring. He dutifully played the two scenes they asked him to read for the director and producer—even letting them suggest alternative readings and playing their game. But he did not connect with the material he was reading and he had the feeling that the decision makers who sat behind the table—all of whom seemed to be about twenty-two years old—had stopped listening after about five minutes. He was angry no one had bothered to send him a script in advance and made a mental note to give his agent a call tomorrow and vent his anger.

Steve Meza was a dark, extremely good-looking young man who had been raised in the barrio of East Los Angeles. In high school he had been bored by sports and—at the urging of a friendly English teacher—had tried out for the school play. He got the part and was soon bitten by the acting bug, appearing in three productions before he graduated. In junior college he continued taking acting and technical theater classes. He finished at L.A. City College and moved on to the theater program at UCLA. Though he never got a degree, he spent a year learning all he could and then moved on to doing part-time jobs and trying to break into the acting world.

He had a few successes, got an agent to represent him, and was now desperately trying to build his career. It was tough but he was driven to make it and didn't mind waiting on tables as long as it gave him the opportunity to work on his acting by doing little theater productions and going out to read for jobs whenever his agent sent him.

He had met Rogers Kennison at UCLA. Their relationship had become a close and intimate one in a short time and when Rogers finished school, they decided to move in together.

At this moment he was hungry and was pulling some food from the refrigerator when he heard Rogers come in. He could tell by the slam of the door that Rogers had had a bad day too.

Steve moved to the doorway of the kitchen as his roommate dropped into a chair, head in hands.

"Lousy day?"

"Shit, yeah."

"What happened this time?"

"Just another crappy assignment. Some asshole gang member gets blasted in a driveby and I get the nod to go cover the story. I don't know why the hell we even bother to cover this shit. They happen every damn day. Maybe if we just let them alone, they'd kill each other off and we wouldn't have to go through this day after day."

"Easy man, you happen to be talkin' about the neighborhood I grew up in."

"Well it may surprise you to learn that this shooting was in Van Nuys—not your old East L.A. turf."

"Sorry, I just assumed—say, doesn't it give you another angle to report a shooting in the valley?"

"Nah—that's not even a surprise anymore. The goddamned gangs are all over the city now."

He looked up at Steve who still stood in the doorway.

"You didn't ask me about my day, Rog."

"Sorry, Steve. Any luck on the interviews?"

"Nope. But if my agent did any real work for me, maybe I might get lucky. You know, the play has two more weekends. If I can get some industry people to see it, maybe they might consider casting me in something."

"Steve. I've been thinking about looking for another paper to work for—maybe even out of L.A."

"Do you really think there are any jobs other places?"

"I don't know, but this one is getting to me. I feel stifled. If I did move, would you come with me?"

There was another pause.

"Depends, I guess. But I don't think there's much work for actors in Minneapolis or Peoria—much that pays."

"Yeah, I know."

"Look, Rog, I'm just getting started in this business. I don't think I want to take off all of a sudden. I've got an agent—though not one to write home about—but he does get me some interviews. I've done a few plays and some of the people in town know me. I don't want to leave before I've even had a chance to get started."

"You're right, Steve. It isn't fair to ask you to leave now—no matter what I can find. Okay. I'll stick it out at the paper—for a while. Something still might come along."

"You never know."

"Yeah. Some surprise may pop up in my office any day."

"Right. Come on in the kitchen. I'll put some steaks on and you can make a salad."

"Right. Nothing like a good dinner to pull one out of depression."

Rogers rose and put his arm around his companion.

Though the depression would not go away so easily, a good dinner sounded like a good idea—at least as a temporary solution.

27 ❖
A Day in the Desert

DENISE WAS DRIVING. Donald watched the scenery. She had prepared well this time. Food. Water. Even some tools. What the hell. There was no one there. Why not break that chain and drive to the Marikem facility beyond the gate? Something was going on out there.

"So you said you would tell me what this is about. I'm waiting."

"Well, it's a whole series of weird things that happened over the last few months. It started with crazy nightmares that scared the shit out of me and kept coming."

And she proceeded to tell him the details of the dreams. But she did omit one minor item. The face of Richard.

"Then I came across this item on a report I was going over—about Project X-29—the same thing I had noticed in the dream—on the container. So then I went to the file room to find more and that's what led me to Frampton Flats."

"That's where we're going now?"

"Yeah. But I've been out here before. It's really a weird experience. Wait'll you see it. A bona fide ghost town."

"Well, one nice thing about a ghost town. There's usually nobody to bother you."

They had turned off the highway and onto the road to Frampton Flats. Donald recognized it as the road they had taken just a few nights before. Instinctively they both turned when they saw the grove of Joshua trees. The final resting place of Vinny Haas.

From what they could see, nothing seemed different from the night they had buried him. But Donald couldn't resist.

"Sleep well, Vinny."

"I'm sure he's doing that very thing. I just wish I could."

"I don't think you'd like to change places with him."

"No. That's for sure."

They reached the town of Frampton Flats and all was as she had remembered it. Still and quiet. Donald eagerly peered at the houses and stores.

"Have you looked close at them?"

"Yeah. Nothing much to see. Rats. Bugs. Probably rattlesnakes and scorpions. Dust and cobwebs. The people who lived here left some things behind—mostly furniture. But they left in a hurry."

"Who lived here?"

"I guess the people who worked in the Marikem facility."

"Why'd they leave?"

"Your guess is as good as mine on that one."

She drove through the town—slowly so he could see it. Then she turned toward the cemetery.

"This is the surprising thing, Donald. Look over there."

He looked where she pointed and could see the neatly kept graveyard, the painted fence around it, the well kept gravestones.

"Somebody's taking care of this place. That's for sure."

"That was my guess too."

She pulled her car up to the fence and stopped.

"Why you stopping?"

"I want to do some closer exploring."

She was out of the car with a notebook in hand and walking briskly toward the graves. Donald got out and stood by the entrance.

He watched her as she knelt by the graves and copied down the data—the names and dates and anything else that was carved into the simple markers. Donald watched from the fence as she moved from stone to stone.

"Are you going to copy all the stuff on all of them?" he called to her.

"Enough to satisfy me. It'll only take a few minutes."

In a few minutes she stopped and headed back to the car.

They drove past the cemetery and back toward the town.

"How come you're interested in the names of dead people?"

"I'm not sure. But maybe finding out something about this town might help fill in the pieces of information about my nightmares. So, if there are no living people to help me, I'll have to rely on the dead ones."

In a few minutes they had reached the fence and the locked gate. Again she stopped the car.

"I've got some tools in the trunk, Donald. One's a bolt cutter I borrowed from a neighbor. I think we can cut that chain."

"Hey, don't you see that sign? They don't want us in there."

"I seem to recall that you never were too serious about following rules and regulations before this."

"But I've turned over a new leaf, Denise."

"Well, I haven't. So if you won't do it, I will."

She had opened the trunk and was hauling out the heavy bolt cutter and a crowbar. Donald moved to help her. He picked up the tools.

"This will probably do it. If it doesn't, I can maybe snap the chain with the crowbar. Come on. Let's see what we can do."

They moved to the gate and both looked again at the ominous "Keep Out" sign that hung above them. Donald paused.

"What are we doing this for exactly, huh?"

"I don't know, Donald. But there just might be some answers if we can get into the plant down this road. It's worth a try."

"I guess the jail term for trespassing isn't as bad as—well the term for some other things I can think of."

She smiled.

Donald tried to get a grip on the chain with the bolt cutter but the links were too big. And so was the shaft of the padlock. So he put the cutter down and tried to use the crowbar. Denise watched as he struggled. Suddenly she heard a noise from behind them on the road. The crunch of boots in the sand. Donald was too busy to notice but Denise turned as she heard it.

"Donald!"

Quickly he turned.

On the road behind them stood a man. He was old and his clothing was rough but the thing that registered most clearly was the fact that he was aiming a shotgun at Donald—a shotgun that was cocked and ready to be fired.

28 ❖
Population of One

NO ONE SAID ANYTHING. Not the man or Donald or Denise. What could you say? They were trying to break into a place they had no business entering. And the man was apparently about to shoot them.

He wore a faded denim shirt soaked with sweat and dungarees worn and patched. He must have been seventy or so and his long gray hair hung to his shoulders. A stubble of beard covered his cheeks, and his skin was weather-worn and tanned from the desert sun.

As Denise watched him, he wiped his mouth with the back of one hand. Slowly he spoke, his eyes riveted on Donald.

"Just drop that there crowbar, mister."

Donald did as requested.

"Now both of you move over there away from the gate."

He gestured with the barrel of the shotgun and they moved to where he indicated.

"This here's private property. The sign makes that pretty damn clear, don't you think?"

Denise had to try something. Who knows what the old man had in mind.

"I work for the company that's in there—Marikem."

"What d'you do for them?"

"Uh—research."

"How come you don't have a key to the lock—like the others that come here?"

Donald chimed in.

"We forgot it. We had to get into the plant. And they can always fix the lock."

"Got any I.D.?"

Denise pointed to the car. "In my purse—there on the seat."

"Git it then."

The man watched her closely as she pulled her purse from the car and fished for the identification card. She handed it to the man and he looked at it closely.

"Well nobody said anythin' about you comin' here. So I can't let you in there until I give them a call to check it out."

"Sure," Denise was too obviously confident. "Make the call."

"You two come with me."

Again he gestured with the shotgun and the three of them began trudging down the road.

Denise volunteered, "We could take my car."

"Just leave the car here for now. It ain't far."

They had gone perhaps fifty yards when he told them to follow a narrow road to the right. There was a small house a short distance from the road—one Denise had not noticed before. It was not in the town proper but sat closer to the plant entrance.

"The door's open."

They filed into the house: Denise, then Donald, the gun, and the man.

To say the place was modest would have been a supreme overstatement. A table and some chairs, a small stove and tiny refrigerator, a narrow bed in the corner—and that was it. The walls desperately needed a coat of paint, but several pictures hung around the room in an attempt to brighten the drab surroundings and there was an official-looking citation hanging beside the door. There must have been a bathroom since Denise noticed a door near the bed that was closed, and another door, slightly ajar, revealed some minimal clothing hanging in a closet.

This was spartan living. Apparently this old man was some sort of a caretaker—probably the one who maintained the cemetery since there wasn't much else to do out here. There was indeed a telephone. And he was intending to use it to verify their credentials.

Denise realized that nobody would vouch for her—whoever he called—and the next step would probably be a call to the police and then, well, whatever the punishment was for trespassing. What a mess.

Damn her curiosity.

He had the phone in hand and was punching in some numbers.

Casually Donald spoke. "Is that your wife who's buried here, Mr. McAvoy?"

The old man stopped and put the phone down.

"How did yuh know that?"

"We saw all the gravestones."

Denise was wondering how Donald knew so much but a closer look showed her the official-looking document on the wall was a certificate of commendation, and she realized Donald was holding the pad she had used to write down the names copied from the grave markers.

Denise tried an approach. "Did she work for Marikem long?"

"Ten years." His response was introspective and said with a sigh.

"When did she die?"

"A year ago—when the others did."

"The others?"

"The ones buried over in the graveyard."

Suddenly Denise realized something that had not registered as she copied the data from the markers in the cemetery. While the birthdates varied, almost all these people had died in the same year—last year. What kind of a grotesque coincidence could this be?

The old man came out of his reverie.

"I dunno what you two are doin' here, but I think you better git out. My job's keepin' this place clear of strangers 'cause they don't want anyone snoopin' around. Now git before I call the cops—or the security guys."

Again he leveled the gun at them, this time swinging it toward the door.

Realizing they had been given a chance they hadn't anticipated, Denise and Donald moved quickly toward the door. The old man stood in the doorway and watched as they trudged up the road back to the car, turned it around and headed out of Frampton Flats as the dust billowed up behind them.

29 ❖
More Questions than Answers

THEY WERE MOVING ALONG the dusty road that led to the highway. Denise was driving and trying to sort out some of what had happened that day. Suddenly she turned to Donald.

"That was pretty smart of you back there—getting us out of that situation."

"Thanks. Y'know you dropped that pad when you were fumbling for your ID to show that guy. I picked it up and just happened to be hanging on to it when we got into his shack. Then I saw that certificate on the wall and recognized the name from your list—and, well, the rest was just playing an angle."

"Not bad."

"Lucky for us it touched a nerve—talking about his wife. That's what saved our asses."

"He also told us something I hadn't thought of, too. All the people in that cemetery died the same year. I wonder what happened."

"I never heard anything. You'd think some disaster like that would be in all the papers."

"You'd think so. But there are things that happen that don't get much coverage. I think I've got enough now to start some intensive research and maybe I can get some answers."

She had reached the highway and turned—with a screech—onto the main road. They headed back to town in silence, each immersed in trying to sort out some order from the chaos.

As they reached the outskirts of the city, Donald suddenly turned to her.

"Say, why don't we head toward—"

"—the library."

And they both remembered how—all through their married life—this had been a favorite running gag. They would finish each other's sentences. Their minds would follow such similar paths that it was almost as if each would read the other's mind. Now they were doing it again. And they both broke into laughter.

"Jesus, Denise, we're still doing it, aren't we?"

"I guess great minds run in the same stupid channels—as somebody once said."

"But doesn't that mean something?"

"Just that we could do a circus act—if we run out of other occupations."

"I always thought it meant we were—always kind of on the same wavelength."

"In some things, Donald—just in some things."

She had pulled into the parking lot of the central library, and as they moved up to the imposing structure, they could see from the sign (a new sign recently added in response to budget cutbacks) that they had just over an hour before the building closed. It was a building that had been built in the twenties and a new proposal to refurbish it had just been passed. It was sorely needed. They moved down the halls that bore the distinct stench of urine and into the periodicals room. At the desk Denise requested the microfiche cards for all of last year's editions of *The News-Telegram*. The librarian cautioned them that their time was limited and Denise assured her they would be finished in a few minutes (or so she hoped).

They worked together. The microfiche cards were divided between Denise and Donald. She had January to June; he had July to December. They sat together at two readers and patiently inserted the plastic cards, scanning the pages of the previous year.

News events half remembered panned by, ads for everything tempted Denise to stop and she had to force herself to recall that all this was history. All the clothing sales and food bargains were now in the past. She had missed her chance many months ago.

And then she saw it. A tiny item on page 24.

She read the details of the article but could hardly believe what it said.

Accident at Test Facility

by Rogers Kennison

> A spokesman for Marikem Industries reported yesterday that a chemical leak at the Frampton Flats Test Facility had occurred. Several injuries to workers at the plant were observed but there were no fatalities.
>
> Authorities are investigating the cause of the accident but so far no specific information is available.
>
> The spokesman said that all care has been taken to control the leak and there is no danger to residents in the area.

And that was all.

Denise read the brief piece several times incredulously. Then she blurted out quite audibly, "God-damned liars!"

Several heads turned her way—including Donald's—but all quickly returned to their own researches. Donald rolled his chair over next to her and read the small notice.

"Can you believe that?"

"At this point I think I can believe almost anything."

"Maybe there's a follow-up story," he suggested.

So she eagerly continued scanning the pages via the viewer, but could find nothing. Day after day. Nothing. They had seen the cemetery, the deserted town, the locked plant gate with its threatening sign, and the man with the gun. Yet no one else seemed to be aware of it. It seemed impossible to believe. All those dead and no report of it?

Donald was thinking again and she was impressed.

"There's a reporter's name on that excuse for a story."

She panned back to the page.

"Rogers Kennison."

"Well, if he's still with the paper, maybe—"

"—maybe," she finished," we should try to look him up."

And, remembering to make a copy of the page, they returned the microfiche sheets, and headed toward the door.

Donald, however, made a quick stop at the phone by the entrance, flipped through the directory pages, and copied down the address of the *News Telegram*.

It always helped to know where you were going.

30 ❖
Slow Newsday

ON SATURDAYS THE *News-Telegram* offices lacked the bustle of activity the casual observer might notice during the week. Newspapers do come out every day and stories need to be written to fill those awkward spaces between the advertisements, but on the weekend, the traditionally frantic journalistic pace seemed somewhat muted.

The *News-Telegram* occupied most of an old building in the downtown area. It was a structure that had been built in the 1950's and now showed definite need of refurbishing. Even the letters of the sign affixed to the side of the building were weather-worn and badly needed to be repainted.

Denise and Donald stood in the lobby scanning the directory but the name they were looking for was not there. Either Rogers Kennison was no longer with the paper, or—more likely—he wasn't important enough to be listed in the pantheon of editors and assistant editors whose names graced the wall.

In the corner of the lobby a uniformed guard sat listlessly behind an imposing bank of video monitors, eyeing them as they went over the directory. When their search produced no results, Denise and Donald approached him.

"May I help you folks?"

"We're looking for a reporter—Rogers Kennison."

The guard pulled out a loose-leaf binder and flipped through the computer-printed pages.

"Yep, he's here."

"We'd like to talk to him."

"I'll check if he's in."

He picked up the phone and punched in a couple of numbers. There was a pause—and then someone answered.

"This is Max at the front lobby. There's a couple of people here to see you."

He looked at Denise.

"Names?"

"Uh—Denise and Donald Burton. Tell him we're from Marikem Industries. It's a—about a story he did about one of our test facilities."

The guard dutifully relayed the information—almost getting it correct. There was another—still longer—pause.

"Okay, I'll send them up."

Denise looked at Donald. Apparently the company name meant enough to gain them entry to the inner sanctum of the newspaper office.

"He's in 502. Take the elevator to the fifth floor. You'll find it."

But finding Rogers Kennison was easier said than done. As they stepped off on the fifth floor, they were confronted with a large room with numerous cubicles—most of which were deserted. The place actually did resemble the busy city room made popular in movies and TV shows whenever a typical newspaper office was shown. But there was nothing resembling a room 502.

Donald stopped a young woman moving rapidly toward the elevator.

"We're looking for room 502."

"Just walk through the city room. It's on the other side—on your right."

They moved through the room and eventually found the door they were looking for. Evidently Mr. Kennison had some status. Most of the reporters worked at their word processors amid the bustle of the city room. He had his own private cubicle.

Denise tapped at the door and a voice called for them to come in.

The office was little more than a cubby hole and almost every available space was piled with papers, folders, magazines, and newspapers. The desk was covered, a side table was covered, the two chairs in the room were covered, and most of the floor was covered.

It looked as if no space had been left untouched. A large bulletin board on one wall was covered too, with clippings, announcements, memos, pictures—and here also there was no available space and many items covered other items which probably covered other items as well. Even the computer screen on the desk gave evidence of the same clutter. Post-it notes and taped on messages hung all around the screen—which was on and showed a story the reporter was currently working on.

They introduced themselves and Kennison cleared the debris off the two chairs.

"Look, I'm sorry, but I've only got a few minutes to talk—I'm on a deadline and the story's only about half done. So I'd really appreciate it if you folks'd make it quick, huh?"

Kennison was younger than Denise had expected—probably in his mid thirties, she thought. Today he was definitely dressed for comfort: an open shirt, slacks, and sandals hanging on his bare feet.

Denise came to the point.

"You did a story last year about the Marikem accident— the one at Frampton Flats. Was there ever any more information on what happened?"

Kennison thought for a minute.

"Hmm. Yeah, I remember that story. I think the company came out with a press release that covered almost everything. We sent a reporter out—I think I was too busy at the time— and he interviewed someone at the plant."

Denise cut in, "Did you ever go to Frampton Flats?"

"I didn't. But I know somebody went out there. The TV people covered it too."

"And no one did any more investigation at all?"

"Look, Miss, there was a minor accident at the plant and a couple of people got hurt. That's not what we call a major story, you know."

Denise could sense the sarcasm and recognized he was under pressure. She had to get his attention.

"Mr. Kennison, there *is* a major story at Frampton Flats. There are a lot of very dead people there, the plant has been shut down totally, and a number of very strange things are going on out there that I'm sure the public would like to know about."

Kennison's brash demeanor changed. The peremptory attitude they had encountered when they walked in suddenly vanished. His reporter's antenna had gone up and he sensed that these two who had interrupted his story might have something that might be truly juicy—if, of course, there was some truth to what they had said. (He did get calls from three or four crackpots almost every week.)

"Mrs. Burton, have you been out there recently?"

Donald cut in, " We just came from there."

"And?"

"There's a cemetery out there with more than fifty recent graves—and I think most of them were victims of that 'minor' accident you reported about."

There was a pause.

"How come you know about this?"

Denise decided that nightmares did not make good newspaper copy so she said, "I work at Marikem, and—well—let's say a series of events led me to do a little investigation."

He was jotting down notes now.

"What do you do at Marikem?"

"I'm in charge of a typing section, Mr. Kennison. But I have some access, occasionally, to information about—well, various things."

"What do you think is going on out there?"

"I'm not sure. But whatever it is, the company wants to keep it very quiet."

"So why did you come to me? You could probably lose your job if they found out, you know."

"Maybe. But somehow, I seem to be involved in all this—I'm not even sure exactly how. And I'm desperately trying to find out some answers. I figured maybe you could help."

"I'll get right on it. Why don't you give me a number where I can reach you and I'll call you as soon as I do some checking on this."

She gave him her phone number and she and Donald got up to leave.

Kennison shook their hands and opened the door for them.

"I'll keep in touch," he said. He took out a card and jotted something on it and handed it to her as they moved into the hallway.

By the tone of his voice, Denise sensed that he truly meant what he said.

31 ❖
Recurring Habits

THEY DROVE BACK TO HER apartment in silence. Denise was trying to understand exactly what was going on but too many pieces of the puzzle were still missing. Finally Donald broke the quiet.

"Do you think that reporter can do anything?"

"I hope so. But Marikem is pretty damn strong. If they could keep all those deaths a secret, who knows what else they can do."

"But those press guys love to expose corruption—any kind of cover up. Look at Watergate and the Iran-Contra thing—"

"Sure. Those are the stories that got out. But I'll bet there are dozens of others that never got exposed. Look how long it took to find out about all those horrible radiation tests they did on people back in the fifties and sixties."

"Well, if there's good material on this one, it'll get out. What d'you want to do now?"

"I'm not sure. I'd love to find out more about what's going on at Marikem. Maybe Richard—the guy I'm seeing—can give me some answers. He knows a lot about that place. But so far he's hardly said anything. He claims it's all security stuff."

"Then don't count on getting anything out of him. I can't understand how you can be interested in a guy who won't talk."

"Oh, he talks. But not about his job."

"And he's probably cute, too?"

"Good looking is how I'd put it."

"You always thought I was, too."

"I still do, Donald."

She saw a smile creep over his face, and the hope that always seemed to spring eternal in Donald. Donald, the perennial romantic.

"But that," she quickly interjected, "doesn't mean we have a future together. I appreciate all you've been doing, but you do owe me, considering all the shit I went through for all those years."

"Okay, okay, Denise. But I feel somehow more like the way it was back at the beginning of our relationship. We're doing things together—helping each other—"

"But that's a lot different than being married, Donald. A lot different."

They were silent again as she pulled up in front of her apartment.

"Want some dinner?" she asked him.

"Sure."

And just like in the old days she pulled a frozen casserole dish from the freezer, popped it into the microwave, and started cutting up some vegetables for a salad as Donald set the table.

She was clearing the table and Donald was on the phone in the bedroom. Times like these made her think about the (outside) possibility of their renewing the relationship. They worked together well—a team—thinking the same thoughts (almost), complementing each other. Donald came into the kitchen.

"I've got to go out for a while."

"What is it?"

He didn't want to say, but immediately she suspected. One of his "deals." One of his old buddies wanted him to do something and he was going to oblige.

"Can I use your car, Denise?"

"You're at it again, Donald. I know."

"No—it's just a little favor—for a friend."

"Drugs?"

"No. Absolutely not. No drugs. I'm through with all that. Honest."

She offered the keys, feeling that there really was no end to the agony of Donald Burton. Who knows what he was getting into this time. He declined the offer, holding up his own copies.

"I'll be back in a couple of hours."

"Sure. Just don't wreck my car, huh?"

"Don't worry, Denise. I"ll take good care of it."

It must have been about 10:30 and she was dozing in front of the TV.

The gentle purr of the phone awoke her.

She was expecting to hear Donald's voice and some tale of woe—she hoped her car was still in one piece—but there was a pleasant surprise.

"Denise—it's Richard."

"Richard! I thought you were out of town."

"I was. But I got back earlier than I expected. Can we get together—tomorrow?"

"Okay."

"How about lunch?"

"Fine."

"I'll pick you up at noon."

"I'll be right here."

It was indeed a nice surprise. Now maybe she could get some answers from him about Marikem—at least some clues. After all, as intimate as they were—he could at least confide in her with some details about his job. She'd make a try at it. Maybe she might find out a few things at least.

32 ❖
Luncheon Date

DONALD (AS SHE EXPECTED) did not come back that night. Denise, however, had a nightmare-free sleep and that made her feel good enough to ignore the fact that Donald—and her car—were out there somewhere—who knows where. She really should have quizzed him more about where he was off to, but every time their relationship moved along well, she forgot about the bad times. She got suckered in until— boom—he did another stupid thing and she ended up paying for it—one way or another.

He called about ten to reassure her that the car was okay—and so was he. He still wouldn't supply much in the way of explanation, but she was able to find out from him that a "friend" was having trouble with his wife and he had gone over to help. Apparently the domestic squabble had escalated to genuine violence when he got to their house and he had extricated the man and spent the rest of the night driving around to cool him down.

Donald—a marriage counselor? This was hard to believe. If he *was* telling the truth, this was certainly a new role for him. Come to think of it, she thought, you don't necessarily need to have success with your own marriage in order to advise others. The counselor she and Donald went to when they were trying to "save" their marriage had admitted she herself was divorced. At the time Donald had been skeptical, but in retrospect, maybe it helped to experience a bad marriage before you could advise others. Maybe that way you could be sensitive to which couples were not going to make it.

At eleven Edie called and Denise had to beg off talking to her by explaining she had a lunch date with Richard. Surprised he was back, Edie began her usual questioning, but Denise soon cut the conversation short, explaining she had to get herself ready.

He arrived promptly at twelve and when she saw him at the door, she felt a warm glow. He moved directly to her and kissed her passionately in an embrace they held for a long time. Finally, he pulled away with a smile—

"We do want to go to lunch, don't we?"

"I think so."

"We'd better. I'm starved."

Again he had picked a tiny, charming place, this time in Santa Monica. It had a garden patio bedecked with flower pots that hung from above and chamber music playing on the speaker system. The ambience was perfect for a Sunday brunch and the waiter uncorked a small bottle of champagne as a fitting opening to the meal.

The champagne buoyed her spirits and the French bread was warm and crusty. They had salads and marvelous poached salmon. It was all delicious and exquisitely served and the bubbly wine heightened the total effect.

They watched each other as they ate and she realized that he had only been away for a few days but she missed him— missed him terribly.

A Schubert quartet was playing in the background as they sipped a delicious coffee blend (specialty of the house). Denise had said nothing about her activities of the previous day and Richard was his usual quiet self. They were reveling in the wine, the food, and each other. Finally she spoke—but she started cautiously.

"Richard, do you know anything about something going on at Marikem—called Project X-29?"

There was a hint of surprise on his face as he looked up from his coffee but he managed to control it and responded casually.

"Why do you ask?"

"Oh—something I came across when I was copying some reports. It, well, it looked kind of interesting."

"I've heard something about it, but it's not really in my department."

"What have you heard?"

"Oh, there's some facility out in the desert where they did some special testing a while back."

"Frampton Flats?"

"Yes. How did you know that?"

"It was on the report."

"Do you know any more about it?" He was very serious now.

"Not much. Do you know what went on out there?"

"Very little. Why do you want to know?"

"I'm not sure but you know those nightmares I was telling you about?"

"Yes."

"Something about this project and Frampton Flats seems tied to the nightmares."

"That's strange."

"I thought so, too. Do you think you could find out more about this Project X-29 for me?"

"Possibly. But the company's very tight on information when it comes to projects you're not involved with. I might talk to some of the other lab people."

"I'd really appreciate it."

They were silent for some time. She decided to wait before telling him about her own visits to Frampton Flats—at least until he could tell her a bit more. He would probably get annoyed if she told him she had gone there and there would be time enough for that.

Finally he said, "Do you think the psychologist you're seeing is helping at all with the nightmare problem?"

"I don't know. I've only seen him twice. He may prescribe something for me or try hypnosis."

"Have they been as frequent?"

"It varies. But here's something I don't think I told you. Guess who was in the last one? You!"

"Me?"

"Yep. And you were playing a pretty sinister role, if you ask me."

"What was I doing?"

"You were one of the doctors in the surgery room."

"Really?"

"But don't worry, everybody seems to feel that getting reality into your dreams is a very common thing."

"I guess I should feel honored. Maybe it means I've reached an important place in your life."

"Who knows?" She smiled.

He paid the check and they walked slowly to his car.

It was after two when they reached her house and she noticed her car was still not back.

Donald was still gone but who knew when he would come popping in. She wasn't quite sure how to handle it if Richard wanted to come up, but when they stopped, he leaned over and kissed her.

"I hope you'll understand, Denise, but I've got a lot of paper work to clean up before I go into the office tomorrow and I'm afraid I'll be up late getting it done. So, if you don't mind, I'll say goodbye."

"No problem." He had solved her problem, too.

He kissed her again and she got out, waved goodbye, and watched him move off down the street.

She was not sure if his ardor had cooled since he had walked in at noon or whether his job was really intruding and he did have a heavy evening ahead of him. But it had been a lovely lunch and she doubted if she would be hungry for any dinner as she climbed the stairs to her apartment.

There was one message on the answering machine. Donald was again reassuring her all was okay and he—definitely—would be back that night—but probably late.

Denise rattled around the apartment looking for something to read but there wasn't much. She could call Edie but that would just mean another interrogation and she wasn't in the mood. She looked outside. It was a pleasant day so she decided to take a walk. She was feeling good and she could use the exercise.

33 ❖
Two New Visitors

THREE PEOPLE SAT AROUND the table in the kitchen of Gerry Gotschalk's little bungalow. It was Sunday and Gerry and his wife Rhonda had intended to take their three year old son to the park for a quiet picnic, then get her mother to babysit for the evening so they could see a movie. Now the little boy sat in the front watching TV while Gerry, Rhonda, and Rogers Kennison sipped coffee.

"It'll only take a few hours, Gerry. We'll be back by five."

"And what about our picnic? I've been promisin' Tod we'd take him to the park all week. I haven't had a chance to be with him for weeks now. You're screwin' up my plans, Rog."

Rhonda said nothing. She was a striking black woman who generally went along with Gerry's plans. He was a good provider and cared about her and the little boy. But his work schedule often left him with little free time.

"Listen, Gerry, this may be a really big story. I did some research on Marikem and it looks like the guy who runs the place may have pulled some slightly irregular deals over the years. Nobody's proved anything but he's been getting sweetheart contracts with the government for a long time. I have a gut feeling there may be a lot to expose—if we can get some hard facts."

Gerry looked at his wife. She shrugged.

"This may be a break for both of us, Gerry. Please come with me. You won't regret it."

Rhonda looked into the room where the little boy watched the flickering cartoons. "I'll take him to the park,

Gerry. Maybe you'll be back in time for dinner and we can head for MacDonald's. Tod'll like that."

Rogers turned to her. "Thanks, Rhonda. This could be important for Gerry and me."

Now Kennison's little Toyota was bouncing along the bumpy road to Frampton Flats.

"So what exactly do you expect us to find out here, Rog?"

"Well, it's a hunch—based on what some people told me yesterday and it just could be a doozey of a story."

"That's what you always say. I don't know why I listen to you on these crazy after-hours jobs. Why can't you just stick to the stuff your assignment editor gives you, huh?"

"Because I never get the good, juicy stuff. If I want to make a name for myself on that rag, I've got to get out and do something they'll notice."

"Well I hope your instincts are good because you're sure fucking up my day."

"Don't worry, Gerry, I think this may be more fascinating than a picnic in the park."

They could see the town up ahead and in a few minutes they had reached the abandoned buildings that constituted the center of Frampton Flats.

Kennison was out of the car, tape recorder in hand, walking by the desolate buildings, dictating what he was observing. Gotschalk had his camera out and was busily snapping images of the surroundings.

"What do you think, Gerry?"

"Not much. Pretty much like a lot of ghost towns I've shot. Some of them have a lot more character."

"But have you ever seen one as modern as this—like it was abandoned just days or weeks ago."

"So?"

"Well, I know they had an accident at the plant here last year."

"So what? They closed down the place, I guess, and the people moved out."

"Come on. There's another spot I want you to get some shots of."

They were back in the car heading for the cemetery Denise had described to him.

But from a slight rise in the terrain they were being observed.

An old man in faded dungarees and worn flannel shirt watched the Toyota and its occupants as it rumbled toward the well-kept graveyard. In a few minutes he had returned to the shack he lived in and was punching in a phone number that was scrawled on a scrap of paper tacked up above the telephone.

Kennison and his photographer were by now walking amongst the grave markers. Again the reporter was describing what he saw into his recorder while Gotschalk was busily snapping away at the graves.

"She was right about just about everything—including these graves."

"What about them?"

"The dates. Aren't you watching?"

"Watching what?"

"Just about all of these people died the same year—last year. The damned company reported there were no major injuries caused by the accident."

"A real coincidence, huh?"

"Right."

They were back in the car now and had turned around and were headed back to the city. Gotschalk was unimpressed.

"So what's the whole damn thing prove?"

"Not much yet, but tomorrow I can talk to my editor and I think I've got enough here to do a lot more digging. I'll see what the Marikem people have to say and maybe insist they let me into the abandoned plant. They have a lot of questions to answer about this whole thing and I intend to get to the bottom of it."

They had been at the town for perhaps two hours and, as they bounced along the poorly kept road leading back to the main highway, the sun was setting, giving a rosy cast to the sky and the occasional yucca bushes and Joshua trees they passed.

Rogers Kennison was deep in thought plotting a strategy on how to handle this story—a story he felt could be a major bombshell if he did it right. His mind was flashing to a whole series of articles, maybe a magazine piece and—who knows—it might mean a book and possibly lots more.

Gerry Gotschalk was cleaning his equipment, marking the film cannisters, and repacking his bags.

Both had forgotten to buckle their belts.

Both of them also failed to notice the car behind them. The car that was rapidly closing the distance and soon would be almost on their tail. And when Kennison finally became aware that they were being followed, it was too late.

The large, black Mercury had reached them and was starting to pull around to the passing side. Kennison floored the accelerator urging his little car onward but it was giving him all it was capable of and in minutes the other car was next to him. Kennison could see nothing through the tinted windows of the Merc but he knew he was in trouble as it started nudging him to the right—nudging him off the road. He hit the brake to slow but it was too late for that maneuver.

The other car had made scraping contact with his front fender—he heard the shriek of metal and he knew he was headed off the road, his little Toyota skidding on the sand of the shoulder.

"Hang on," was all he could yell to his passenger as they skidded helplessly into the underbrush of scrub and cactus, his tires spinning wildly in the sand, his car turning, turning. And suddenly—ahead of him—loomed the grotesque image of a Joshua tree. And in an instant—as he tried to make the brakes work—the car slammed headlong into the misshapen tree.

34 ❖
No News Can Be Bad News

IT HAD BEEN A GRUELING day at work. Hillman was pushing all the typists to get reams of work out and Denise had to keep on top of it all. Edie asked her to talk to him and suggest that they could at least hire some temp workers. She talked to him at the break. Hillman said he would take her suggestion under advisement and proceeded to dole out even more assignments to everyone in the room.

They all left the office tired, dreading the rest of the week if it proved to be anything like this excruciating Monday.

At home, Denise pulled off her clothes, slipped on some shorts, a baggy tee-shirt, and exchanged her heels for some old sandals. At least she could be comfortable in spite of her fatigue.

Donald had gone off again—thankfully without her car this time. She flopped down on the bed wondering what to do about her dinner.

Suddenly she thought about the interview they had had with Kennison. If he really was serious about the Marikem story, he should have done something about it by now.

She got up quickly, rummaged in her purse for the business card he had given her and called the newspaper. No one answered at his extension number. Some reporter! Then she idly turned the card over and discovered what he had scrawled on the back—his home number. She tried it (what the hell).

A man's voice answered.

"Is this Mr. Kennison?"

"No."

"Is he there?"

"No. Who is this?"

"I spoke with him a few days ago—about a story."

"Oh. Well—Rogers has been in an accident. He ran off the road in the desert last night. He's in pretty bad shape at Fuller Memorial."

Denise gasped audibly.

"Was he alone?"

"No. There was a photographer with him. He's in bad shape too."

Off the road? In the desert? How could anyone . . . ?

"Can he see visitors?"

"No. He's in Intensive Care. Who is this?"

"My name's Denise Burton. Who are you?"

"I'm Steve—Rog's—uh—roommate."

Hmm. Probably a bit more than that, Denise thought.

"I'm going to see him tomorrow. I'll mention you called, okay?"

"Yes. Thanks. I sure hope he's gonna be okay."

"Yeah. Well, if you pray, you might spend some time on Rog. He's gonna need it in the next few days."

And he hung up.

Denise fell back on the bed. Christ! What was going on? He had gone out after the story at Frampton Flats and had ended up almost dead. Was she responsible? What the hell was happening? Was it an accident or was somebody playing hardball? Yet she had been out there and nothing had happened to her.

She heard her door open and jumped up nervously, but it was only Donald.

"Hi, Denise. Boy, you sure seem jittery. What's going on?"

She told him.

They both sat there for a long time after Denise finished. Quietly. They were stunned that someone out there was deadly serious—serious enough to try to kill to keep things quiet. And there was the unspoken aspect. It could have been them. They could have been the ones lying shattered in a hospital at this moment—or in the morgue.

Donald spoke first. "It could've been an accident, you know."

"Sure. I don't know much about the details, but I'm willing to bet it was no accident."

"How could anyone know who they were—or even that they were there?"

"The old guy—the one who stuck his shotgun in our faces. I'm sure he keeps his eyes out for anyone. And Kennison took a photographer with him so it was kind of obvious what was going on."

"So what now?"

"Well, I don't know about you, but I intend to go back out there and talk to that old guy because that may be the only way I can get more information."

"Are you kidding? You're liable to end up in Intensive Care along with those other two guys."

"I've been out there twice, Donald, and nothing's happened to me."

"You'll be pushing your luck, Denise."

"Well, maybe so. But remember when we were in the old guy's shack? What was it that got to him—"

"His wife." Again he read her thoughts.

"Maybe—just maybe—we can appeal to him again. He does have a sensitive spot."

"He also has a very imposing shotgun."

"It's probably not even loaded."

"I prefer not to find that out the hard way."

"Lighten up, Donald. For a guy with some very sleazy friends, you certainly are scared of a little adventure. What about the old days, huh? We used to do a lot of wild and adventurous stuff then."

"Well, these days I've decided to live a more careful life. But I'll do it for you. When do you want to go?"

"Tonight's as good a time as any, don't you think?"

"I tend to prefer daylight myself."

"Well, I don't want to waste any more time. Look, if you won't go with me, I'll go by my lonesome."

"Okay. You win. But this time, I intend to be a bit more prepared."

He opened a kitchen cabinet and reached far into the back behind some utensils Denise rarely used. Wrapped in a dish towel, he withdrew the shiny metal revolver that he and Vinny had struggled over not too many days before—the revolver Denise knew too well.

"I decided not to get rid of this. It might prove to be helpful—just in case."

Denise was skeptical. "You're just going to get us both killed, Donald."

"I'll keep it in the car. But the old guy has his artillery and I want some protection too."

"Okay," she relented, "but I'm not sure I like the idea."

They took off for the desert, not even realizing neither one of them had eaten any dinner. On the way, the hunger pangs hit both of them so they pulled over at a roadside coffee shop and had sandwiches and coffee—at least enough to fortify them for awhile.

By nine they had reached Frampton Flats, and, as in the past, all was quiet and dark.

Denise drove directly to the shack they had exited from in haste on their last visit. They tried to be casual and definitely un-secretive and pulled up (maybe too boldly) directly in front of the little building. In a minute he was there—standing in front, shotgun over his shoulder.

35 ❖
A Tale of One City

"SO YOU'RE BACK. What d'yuh want this time?"

"Mr. McAvoy, something happened here last night."

"Them fellas that was takin' pitchers, you mean?"

"Yes."

"Did you send 'em here?"

"Not exactly. But I did talk to them."

"So why'd yuh come back, huh?"

"Those two men are in the hospital—they may die."

McAvoy was quiet. He ran his sleeve across his lips and stared at Denise as she sat in her car.

"You sure o'that?"

"Very sure. And I don't think it was an accident."

"No. Me neither."

Denise looked into the eyes of the old man. She sensed he was genuinely concerned. She took a chance.

"Mr. McAvoy, I do work for Marikem, but I don't like a lot of things they're doing these days."

"Yeah. Me too."

"Could we come in and talk to you about—well, about what's been going on here?"

He looked around, then stooped down to see who was in the passenger seat, grunted at Donald, and gestured for them to come in.

They sat in the little living room of his shack. Two small lamps illuminated the room, throwing bizarre shadows on the wall. He had turned off the tiny TV that threw a flickering blue glow they had noticed when they first came in. It was as sparse as they had remembered it from their last visit and, in the dark, seemed colder and more foreboding.

They talked for a few minutes—about Kennison and his visit. Denise explained a bit more about who she was and what had been happening. McAvoy was silent for a time. Denise wasn't sure if she would be able to get him to talk at all. So she asked about McAvoy's wife. He thought for a while, not responding. Then he took a deep breath, looked closely at Denise and Donald and started to talk.

"You folks know m'name. McAvoy. Varny McAvoy. I've lived out here at the Flats for close on forty year now. Me and Betsy—m'wife—moved out here back in the fifties—t' get away from the city. We couldn't stand the noise an' the people. I guess we was both used to another kind o'life. Both of us was raised on farms. I was collectin' some disability from a wound in the war and we had some money put away so we headed out here to the desert t'live simple. I could always make some money repairin' cars or machinery an' we didn't really need much.

"We got t'like the desert. Funny thing. Most folks think there's nothin' here. But they's wrong. This place is really alive. The stuff that grows out here is amazin' an' in the spring it's really purty what with the wildflowers an' all. An' there's all kinds a critters that live out here. Y'see them at night, mostly, coyotes and mountain lions an' lots more.

"When we first come here they was only a handful of folks livin' here in the Flats. But things changed when they built the plant.

"Lots more folks moved in and it got busier and busier. It wasn't bad—mind yuh—most of them was good folks an' we all got along.

"After the plant was put up, they wanted folks t'work there, and Betsy, well she figured we could use the money. She could do all them office things—even learned them there computers too—smart woman, that Betsy. So she got herself a job at the plant. An' with more folks in town an' lots more comins and goins I did more repair work—even worked for Maurie's auto repair shop when he needed me. We was doin' well—until the accident."

He stopped and closed his eyes, an old man thinking about the past. But he had reached a sore spot and he had to pause.

Denise waited, then asked, "What happened, Mr. McAvoy?"

He began slowly but gradually became more emotional as the story unfolded.

"It was a little more'n a year ago, I think. Betsy come home an' she wasn't feelin' good. That wasn't like her. I don't think she was sick more'n two or three days all her life. She was real listless, got into bed and just laid there. She wouldn't eat and didn't talk much. It was like the life was goin' out a' her. The company called the next day. They seemed t'know more than we did, an' wanted me to tell 'em all that was happenin' to her. They said they'd send a doctor out that afternoon. An' he come about four with two other scientific types an' all kinds of equipment to examine her.

"They wrote a lot o'stuff down but didn't tell me much except that they'd be back the next day an' they left some medicine that they said would help her feel better, but it didn't do much good. The next day they come back an' examined her again. They said they needed to move her to a bigger place where she could be taken care of better so I signed some papers. She was doin' pretty bad by then an' I wasn't sure what to do. But I found out that she wasn't the only one who was sick. Ed Hathaway's wife, Estelle, was just as bad— she worked at the plant too. And Micky Lubofsky who lived down the street from us then was sick. Later I found out there was lots more too.

"But they couldn't help 'em. They all died. Becky, Estelle, Micky, all of 'em. I never even got to see her in the hospital they took her to.

"They just brought all the coffins back here to bury 'em.

Then they just closed down the plant an' folks moved out—except me. They asked me to stay on an' keep an eye on the place. I didn't want to leave so I said I would."

Again he paused. Denise and Donald had listened carefully. Donald ventured a question.

"And nobody ever said anything about it?"

"We couldn't. They made us sign papers sayin' we wouldn't. It was all security stuff, they said. It had to be kept quiet. We all got paid purty well, too. An' they pay me some to keep my eye out for strangers."

"But you're telling us now—"

"I know, I really shouldn't be but I been thinkin' a lot. That's about all I do these days alone out here. An' then when them fellas was here yestiday—an' I reported it like they told me to—an' what happened. It wasn't right. A lot o'things ain't right. An'—damn it—they can't do anythin' t'me anymore. Not at my age. So I figured I had to talk about it—an' then you folks come along. So I did."

"Do you know what kind of accident it was?"

"Chemicals is all they told us. The plant did experiments with some kinda special chemicals—for defense they said—an' somethin' just went wrong."

"Did you at least have funerals for the dead?"

"Not much. They brought the coffins back here—all closed. They said they was worried about possible infection. There was a nice outdoor ceremony. But that was about all. An' it was all kept quiet. No reporters or TV. An' we all swore we wouldn't talk about it. They said it might hurt us abroad an' all the information was for national defense an' had to be kept from the public."

"And the plant?"

"All sealed up. Now and then they send some folks out to check on it, but it's just about empty. I guess some o' the equipment is still there, an' it's prob'ly not dangerous any more 'cause they don't wear any special suits when they goes in there. But nobody uses it now."

He had stopped talking. Denise had dozens of questions she still wanted to ask but she could see that McAvoy was through. He had told as much as he was going to for now, and she didn't want to pursue it further.

"You folks want some coffee? Water's hot."

She and Donald nodded assent and McAvoy moved off to his little kitchen and came back in a few minutes with three mugs of steaming, black liquid. It was strong and Denise could smell the pungent odor even before he came into the room.

They sipped in silence. Outside there was the stillness of the desert, the stillness that Varny McAvoy loved, the stillness he had come here for. But the desert had destroyed much of what he had loved. Not the desert really, but those who had invaded it, desecrated it, and left a swath of human misery in their wake. In the name of national defense. Who would defend the dead? Or did they have no rights?

Denise pondered these things. Denise Burton, an ordinary hard-working secretary who had somehow gotten entangled in a bizarre series of events leading God-knows-where.

She looked at McAvoy. He too had become entangled in a strange series of events that he had not asked for. In a way, they were two of a kind. But she was different. She was trying to find out some answers. And in spite of all the obstacles, she was finding some.

But she wanted more.

36 ❖
Aunt Vanessa's Friend

IT HAD BEEN ANOTHER EXCITING day. Not exactly fun-filled, but Denise was beginning to develop a real adrenaline high as she pursued this chase—a chase to find answers to her own perplexing nightmares.

She had asked Donald to drop her off at the nursing home where her aunt was. She had not seen her in quite a while and felt guilty, and though there was only an hour left for visiting, Denise wanted to see her. She felt guilty because Vanessa had left a message on her machine—a rather plaintive message—hardly like her at all.

She lay there propped up by pillows, books and magazines littering the bed and a cassette tape playing from the little player on the nightstand. It was Mozart—always Mozart. For Vanessa there was no other composer living or dead but Mozart. Denise could hear the rippling piano even before she entered the room, the touching notes of one of his concertos (she always got them confused no matter what Vanessa told her) and she stood at the door watching her aunt.

When the older woman saw her, she dropped her reading and smiled.

"You got my message, huh?"

"Sure." She moved into the room. "You always know how to get me here."

"Felt guilty, right?"

"Absolutely."

"Well, I finished the book you brought last time. I thought you might want it."

"I'm sure that's why you called."

"Well, it does get kind of lonely here."

"How are you feeling, Vanessa? Honestly."

"Not good. The MS is worse. I'm even feeling it in my arms now. Getting around—even a little—is rough."

"I'm sorry."

"Yeah. Well I knew it was inevitable. But my mind is still sharp. I guess that's kind of the curse of it all. I'm aware of it as it happens. It's a real bitch."

"Sure is."

"What about you, Denise? Still leading a mundane life?"

"The pace has really been picking up in the last few days."

"How come?"

Denise brought her up to date on some of the events that had been happening. She omitted a few details. Sex with Richard—and Donald. And, of course, the killing of Vinny Haas. Some things had to be kept private—even from the astute Vanessa.

"So tell me more about this Richard guy. Is he screwing you?"

"Come off it, Vanessa. Now you're getting too personal."

"You never kept secrets from me in the past, Denise. When you were little, you told me things you wouldn't even tell your parents."

"But I'm not a kid now, Vanessa."

"Exactly. That's what makes secrets all the more intriguing. Besides it's been a hell of a long time since I got laid. Don't deny a horny old woman a little bit of pleasure."

"Well, you could say we've had our intimate moments."

"In other words, you've been fucking."

"Vanessa!"

"I always like to get to the point. It's a good, direct word and I was always fond of it—still am."

Denise wanted to change the subject. So she talked about the visits to Frampton Flats.

"Something's been going on out there, Vanessa, something important and I'm afraid I've gotten pretty deep into it."

"Scared?"

"Hell, yeah. But I can't stop. I need to find out more."

"I say go for it. Say, what about your new boyfriend. Can't he find out some things for you?"

"Richard says he can't get any information. He's really close-mouthed about anything going on at Marikem. I'm just not sure where to go from here."

"Holy shit, I almost forgot. Marcus Kominsky!"

"Who?"

"Doctor Marcus Kominsky. He's an old friend of mine. A very close friend for a while—if I do say so. If anybody can find out stuff about Marikem Industries, Marcus can. He even worked for them for a while—consulting, I think. He's now over at Cal Tech—in Pasadena. I think he still teaches a few classes in chemistry—last I heard. See my address book there by the phone? Look him up and copy down the phone number. I'll bet he knows something—or if he doesn't, he sure as hell can find out for you. Be sure to mention my name. He'll remember me. That's for damn sure."

She flipped through the worn, old book, pages falling out as she turned them, but she found the listing—two numbers in fact, home and the school—and she jotted them down.

Behind her a nurse was tapping at the open door, indicating the visiting time was over.

"Okay, okay, Nellie. Don't get obnoxious."

"I'll go now, Vanessa. Thanks for the information."

"Glad to help. And please keep me informed of what's going on. You know I like mysteries. Almost as much as I like it when you visit, hon."

"I'll try not to make it so long before next time. Bye. And hang in there."

Denise leaned over the bed and kissed her aunt on the cheek.

Vanessa smiled.

"Thanks, Denise, and good hunting."

37 ❖
Academia

SHE HAD EASILY GOTTEN THROUGH on the phone to Dr. Kominsky and Vanessa's name elicited a raucous laugh from the professor. He remembered her well and was eager to find out how she was doing. He was genuinely saddened when Denise explained about her aunt's condition. He agreed to see her the next day—at his office on the campus—even though Denise gave only a suggestion of what she wanted to talk about.

Denise decided that taking a day off (she had plenty of accumulated sick leave) would not be so terrible, and, she felt, she could use a break from the hectic few days she'd been going through.

Finding a place to park on the Cal Tech campus, however, proved a major challenge, but eventually she found a spot—marked "Faculty Only"—and decided to take a chance. She didn't expect to be there too long anyway.

The booming voice of Marcus Kominsky she had heard on the phone did not belie the man in the flesh. He was, as she had expected, large, gray bearded, florid faced and highly effusive.

Denise thought he must be seventy, but he was full of energy and got up to welcome her to his cluttered office in a courtly manner. He offered her some tea and they sat sipping from the steaming cups, not saying much for a few minutes, just idly sizing each other up as they sat in the quiet room.

Kominsky set his cup on the desk—a desk covered with books and magazines and computer print-outs, and spoke first.

"So Miss Burton, you need some advice—I think that's what you said on the phone. I hope it's not marital advice. I'm very poor at that. I've been through three unsuccessful marriages and would never have the courage to make suggestions to other people."

"No. That's not why I came to see you, Dr. Kominsky."

"Please—everyone calls me Marcus."

"Okay. Marcus—my Aunt Vanessa said you had had some contact with the Marikem Company—had done some work for them—I think she said—"

"Yes. I worked for them some years ago. They paid me handsomely and—well—I needed the money. In retrospect, however, I'm not happy about the time I spent there. Ironically, they just recently called me about working there again."

"I work for them now. I'm in charge of a word processing section. But I seem to have kind of stumbled onto something and—well—I need to find out some things."

"Hmm. Before we go any further, I want to tell you a bit about Marikem. These are things I found out after I worked for them and that might have influenced me in making a decision to get involved—if I had known beforehand. But, alas, too many of us have twenty-twenty hindsight."

"What did you do for them?"

"Some consulting on a few chemical projects. It was complicated stuff and they felt I knew more than I really did, but that didn't matter at the time. I helped them work out some problems and they paid me for what I did—as well as for keeping my mouth shut and both of us benefited—I suppose. Of course, they benefited much more than I did. But all this is a tiny slice of history.

"Marikem, Miss Burton, has grown from a very small chemical laboratory—started by a fellow named Mathison about twenty years ago. He named it for his wife, Marissa, taking the first letters of her name—the way a lot of companies get their names, I suppose. She was a lovely woman, from what I understand. She died about fifteen years ago.

"Meredith Mathison, however, is what many of us would refer to as totally unscrupulous. He was a brilliant student at Stanford when he went there. But I think he learned more about manipulating people than about chemistry when he was a student. I hear he never had any trouble getting scholarships and grants to get him through—all the way to a Ph.D. He began working for a small chemical firm in San Jose but he got restless after a few years there. Producing industrial cleaning products was not a career he wanted for the rest of his life.

"This was in the 1950's. The Cold War was happening and the Soviet Union had become our major adversary—at least they wanted us to think so. Mathison was shrewd enough to see that there was going to be a continued build-up of our military forces—as long as the Communist threat loomed on the horizon. So he made some contacts with military people he had met—especially those involved in procurement. Then he manipulated some former classmates—who had some money—into investing in a company he was starting. You have to realize that it was just an idea in his head at this point. But he rented a small facility in San Jose and within a few months Marikem was a reality.

"Mathison is a master of timing. Every new so-called threat provided opportunities for him to expand his chemical development—whether it was the Berlin Wall, the Cuban Missile Crisis, or the Viet Nam War.

"Over the years he's been involved in food additives, compounds for medical use, military cleaning agents, and even gases and biological weapons for the battlefield—though these remain stockpiled, thank God, and have never been used. I hear that Mathison was furious, however, when he lost the contract for napalm to Dow Chemical.

"As you know, Marikem is now a massive operation with government contracts in all areas of chemical experimentation. Mathison very cleverly hires retired officers from the military and they know exactly how to reach the important

Pentagon decision-makers and how to get the very lucrative contracts that enabled him to expand into a highly important and influential company."

"Does the term Project X-29 mean anything to you?"

"No. Not offhand. But remember, I haven't worked there for well over fifteen years now."

Denise felt comfortable with this man. He knew a great deal about Marikem and obviously harbored no love for the company. She decided to tell the whole story and see what Dr. Kominsky could make of it.

So she proceeded to explain the nightmares, her visit to the sixth floor, her chance encounter with the information about X-29, and the subsequent visits to Frampton Flats.

When she finished, Kominsky sat quietly and did not respond. Then he picked up a pad from his desk, pulled a pen from his pocket, and started to jot down some notes—writing feverishly.

"Miss Burton, you must understand that Meredith Mathison has a great deal at stake and will do almost anything to protect his enterprise. He certainly does not want any adverse publicity—especially these days when military work is vanishing and conversion to peacetime projects is where the money is.

"You may well be getting yourself into something that is potentially dangerous to you. I discovered in working at Marikem that these people are not moral. Individual lives mean very little to them. They have an overwhelming doctrine that they alone are aware of some great good they are working toward—and little people—like you and me—are not important. For them, the sacrifice of a few people is easily justified if it furthers a project or experiment. You can't understand these people unless you talk to them and work intimately with them. If anything, I learned as I worked there how the minds of the founders of the Third Reich probably worked. Believe me, some of these people at Marikem would have been very much at home in Hitler's Germany."

Denise was stunned. If what he said was true, she was indeed getting herself—had already gotten herself—deep into territory that was dangerous to her and those around her.

"Then what do you think I should do now?"

"You must stop your investigations before something happens to you. Let me call some people I know and see if I can find out anything about this Project X-29. I'll try to do it this afternoon. But please do not do any more on your own. I mean this seriously. Promise me you won't do any more—at least until we talk again."

She promised and they both rose. The professor extended his hand and she shook it. As she turned to leave the room, he called out, "Tell Vanessa I definitely will phone her. I think she'll be happy to hear a voice from the past."

Denise drove home slowly. All she had done so far had been inspired by curiosity and a kind of reckless energy that drove her to ferret out a mystery that was interrupting her sleep. Like pulling the trigger and killing Vinny Haas—an act she had done virtually without analysis or thought (at the time she couldn't analyze or think), pursuing the answers to Project X-29 had been done impulsively—one thing driving her to another.

Now she had been told—warned—to stop. For her own good. For the first time there was a sense of fear in her. The game had become serious. The stakes had changed. She should have realized this when she found out about Kennison's fate. She was in too deep. But was there really any turning back?

Minutes after she left, Kominsky was checking his address book and punching in a phone number. A female voice answered.

"Hello?"

"Ilona? This is Marcus Kominsky."

"Marcus! It's been such a long time."

"Ilona, I'm sorry. I didn't come to Stuart's funeral."

"I knew you wouldn't, Marcus. I know how adamant you are about things like that."

"You haven't forgotten my little prejudices, have you."

"I know you well, Marcus."

"Ilona, do you have any idea why he did it?"

He could hear her breathing. She was trying to keep control, not to start crying.

"No, Marcus. I honestly don't. There was a note on the computer screen but it didn't say much."

"Do you think it was his job?"

"Possibly. But you knew Stuart. Suicide was not the kind of thing you might expect from him. He was a fighter. When something bothered him, he did something about it. He'd been complaining a lot about Marikem lately but it wasn't something to get him that depressed."

"Do you remember what he was involved in recently?"

"He never told me too much. That was his way. But there was one project called—I think—X-29 or something."

When he finished talking to Ilona Neal, Marcus Kominsky dialed a number he had called just days before. After a bit of tranferring and a few delays—as he suffered with some interminable "easy listening" music—Heinz Lieber picked up the phone.

"Marcus?"

"It's me again, Heinz."

"Always happy to hear from you. Come to any conclusions about our offer?"

"Maybe. Say, any possibility we might meet this afternoon? Can you get free?"

"For you, of course I can. Want to come over here to the lab?"

"No. How about some coffee on my turf? Do you know where Brookside Golf Course is?"

"Sure. Right next to the Rose Bowl, right?"

"There's a restaurant just off the eighteenth hole. Do you know the place?"

"I'll find it."

"How about meeting there about five?"

"Fine. I'll look forward to seeing you again."

It was after noon when Denise got home. There were two messages on her machine. Dr. Glidden's office was calling. He wondered if he could see her that afternoon. He wanted to go over some items and had some new information that he felt might be helpful. The other call was from Rogers Kennison's live-in, Steve. Rogers was showing improvement and might be able to have visitors by the end of the week. His passenger, Gerry Gotschalk, however, was still in intensive care.

38 ❖
The Third Man

DENISE DROVE SLOWLY to Dr. Glidden's office. She thought about the events of the last few days. Two men lay in the hospital seriously injured, and another man who knew a great deal about Marikem had told her in no uncertain terms to stop—to back off. Could she? But more important, was it too late? How much did they (the all powerful "they") know about her and what might they do? Denise Burton, an insignificant secretary, was now an important player in a dangerous game.

She was ushered into Glidden's office and sat opposite the doctor. What could be so important that he had to see her?

"Thank you for coming right over, Miss Burton. I tried to reach you at work but they told me you had called in sick. I hope it's not something serious?"

"Oh, no. Just—an appointment I had."

"Good. I've been going over some of the things we've been covering and the problems with your nightmares and I feel maybe we might try some hypnosis—if you feel comfortable with that."

"Well—I guess so. I've really never done anything like that before."

"Oh, there's nothing to be apprehensive about at all. I'll explain exactly what we'll be doing. I'll basically be giving you what we call post-hypnotic suggestions to help clear your mind and allow you to sleep more peacefully. Are you willing to try it?"

"Okay—if you say so."

"Good. Then we'll make an appointment for our next

session and begin at that time. By the way, have there been any new developments since you were here last?"

Denise felt comfortable with Dr. Glidden, and, having decided to put her treatment in his hands—now with hypnosis as well, decided to tell him about some of the events of the last few days.

She described her visit to Frampton Flats and some of the information she had discovered—that tied in with her nightmares.

She did leave out the visit to the reporter and the subsequent events that happened to him.

Dr. Glidden nodded and asked very few clarifying questions. After about half an hour she had told him much of what had happened to her so far.

"Well, that's about it—up to this point."

"Very interesting. I think you're doing an excellent job trying to find out some of the causal factors producing the dreams. Now we'll start on the hypnosis therapy and soon we may have you back in good shape again. I'm sure you'll be happy to have regular healthful sleep once again, right?"

She agreed, and they shook hands warmly. She made sure to make an appointment for her next visit with the receptionist, and soon she was heading home, feeling hopeful for her future therapy.

Less than an hour after her meeting with Dr. Glidden, three men sat in an office high in the executive tower at Marikem Industries. They included Meredith Mathison, Chief Executive Officer of the company, Otto Gesselman, head of security, and a third—much younger—man. They sat listening to a tape—a tape of the voice of Denise Burton.

They heard her describe (as she just had in person to Dr. Glidden) her attempts to track down the sources of her nightmares and her visit to Frampton Flats.

When she finished, Mathison clicked off the machine.

"Gentlemen, we apparently have a slight problem here."

There was a pause and Gesselman spoke.

"It's not a major problem. I think I can handle it rather quickly and efficiently."

"Perhaps, but there may be a better way." He turned to the third man. "Any thoughts?"

"I don't think Mr. Gesselman needs to get involved. I think I can handle this—for obvious reasons."

Gesselman shrugged. "If you want, it's your baby."

Mathison addressed the younger man, "How soon can we clear it up?"

"I think a day is all I need."

"Good. Gesselman will stay in contact with you if you need any assistance—or any details taken care of. I'll expect to hear from you by the end of the week. Thanks for taking the time to stop by, gentlemen."

The two men rose to go.

Mathison watched them leave. He was a man in command—tall and imposing and in excellent physical condition for his almost seventy years. He had made Marikem what it was and he intended to keep it that way. Minor complications had to be dealt with quickly and his staff was always ready to handle them.

Gesselman had been with him for almost twenty years. He was solidly built, a man who moved with conviction, a man whose bulk filled the doorway as he left the room.

The third man was hardly as imposing. He was younger and seemed almost out of place with these other two. But he seemed just as dedicated to the goals of the company he worked for—just as eager to make sure the goals were accomplished and the company succeeded. He seemed eager to prove himself and move up in the echelons of the Marikem organization. And it appeared he would do almost anything to accomplish these goals.

The third man was Richard Kramer.

39 ❖
Over Coffee

THE RESTAURANT WAS ALMOST DESERTED. The waiters were beginning to set up for the dinner hour and only two or three others sat in the room. From the bar they could hear the happy hour going on—revelers having a few before heading home—hopefully remaining sober enough to negotiate the freeway traffic.

Outside the large picture windows a few late afternoon golfers were finishing their eighteen holes on the adjacent course.

In contrast to Marcus Kominsky's substantial bulk, Heinz Leiber was a small, bespectacled man who talked in a quiet, almost unassuming manner. He was in his sixties, well dressed, his thin gray hair combed neatly, his appearance orderly and tidy. The two presented a sharp contrast even to the casual passerby.

They had exchanged pleasantries, sipped their coffee, and talked about—mainly—unimportant items: mutual friends, former associates.

Finally Leiber ventured the question.

"How about it, Marcus. Want to come over and work with us?"

"I'm thinking about it, Heinz. I really am."

"Well, I guess that's a positive. At least for the moment."

"Of course it is. You know I don't really want to leave teaching. But who knows? They all want me to retire over there and maybe this could be a pleasant change."

"I think you'd like it."

"Anything really interesting going on at Marikem these days?"

"Oh—many things. Some fascinating research projects. We're also branching out into many civilian projects. Humanitarian things—just the sort of projects you care about. Alternative fuels, medical applications—stuff you talked about years ago. Now we have a chance to really work at them."

Marcus Kominsky paused in his reply. He added a touch of sugar to his lukewarm coffee.

"Heinz, do you know anything about a recent project over there called X-29?"

The other man looked carefully at Kominsky.

"Why do you ask?"

"Oh—just a rumor I heard from someone over at Cal Tech. Something that had to do with that test facility out in the desert."

"What did you hear?"

"Not much. Something about an accident out there. Is it true?"

"Yes. There was a minor accident."

"Any deaths?"

"A few—from what I hear. I wasn't really involved much in that project at all. All I know is just hearsay."

"Do you know any more details?"

"Not really. Why the sudden interest?"

"Oh, I just want to make sure that a company I might start working for is an ethical one—you know, honest and aboveboard about what they do."

"Of course. Well, that's all I can tell you about X-29."

"Could you find out more for me if I happened to be interested?"

"I really doubt it. It was a security project. Only those immediately involved in it knew much. I'm sure they wouldn't talk about it."

"Hmm. That's a shame. I've heard some strange rumors

and I'm sure Marikem wouldn't want bad publicity to hurt their name."

"What kind of rumors?"

"Oh, some rather far-out speculation about human experimentation—on live subjects."

He watched Leiber's face, but there was no hint of a reaction.

"Naturally, I don't put any faith in wild rumors like that. I wouldn't want idle gossip to affect any decision of mine. But if you could get some more information about it, well, it might help me make up my mind."

"I can try."

"Good. I'd appreciate it, Heinz."

Then Leiber was on his feet staring at his watch.

"My God, it's almost six. I have a dinner engagement this evening. You will excuse me, Marcus?"

"Certainly." And Kominsky rose and extended his hand.

"It's been good seeing you, Heinz. And I'll certainly look forward to whatever you can find out for me."

They shook and the smaller man made a hasty retreat for the exit. Marcus Kominsky watched him go with a smile.

He doubted if he would hear from Heinz Leiber again.

40
Heavy Date

HER PHONE WAS PURRING as Denise (carefully) unlocked her door. She caught it before her answering machine kicked in.

"Denise? This is Dr. Kominsky—Vanessa's friend."

"Sure. We just talked earlier today. I haven't forgotten you already."

"Listen, I'm doing some checking and I may be able to find somebody who was involved in—in that project we discussed today. I can't say any more on the phone, but I may have a lot more information for you by Monday. Just keep cool—and please don't do anything rash, okay?"

"Okay. I promise to stay out of trouble."

"Good. I'll be talking to you."

She thought maybe taking a nap might be a good way to spend some of the afternoon. She was beginning to feel tired from this ordeal and there had been a good deal of lost sleep over the last few days.

Denise got into bed, taking along a few magazines and was just getting herself comfortable when the purring phone interrupted.

Should she answer it or let the machine do the work? Oh hell, it might be something important.

It was Richard.

"I didn't see you at work today. What happened?"

"Oh, nothing important. I had some appointments. And then the shrink—Dr. Glidden wanted me to come by."

"Feeling okay?"

"Oh, sure."

"Interested in a date tonight?"

"Maybe. Have anything interesting in mind?"

"Possibly."

"Okay. Want to pick me up around seven?"

"Let's make it dinner—I'll come by say six-thirty. Okay?"

"Fine with me."

"I'll look forward to it."

"Me too."

She set her alarm for five, closed the drapes, and put on some soft music. She lay back on the bed and, without even looking at the magazines she had on the bedside table, was soon lulled into a relaxing sleep.

But now the images were swirling, moving in and out of focus.

The corridors, the hospital ward, the operating room.

And then the bodies being dissected.

Now the images zoomed into violent closeups—bloody organs clutched in gloved hands, scalpels slicing into white flesh, gaping incisions, and then—

The figures in the operating room are moving toward her—one holding a massive syringe.

Behind the figure again she sees the others. Again there is Richard's face, menacing, intense, fixating on her.

The image of the needle is now in sharp and vivid closeup. She feels her body held viciously, arms pulled behind her. The needle is closer—closer—and then the sharp stab of pain—and all blurs to melting colors—and—black. Then a buzzing sound—harsh—close. Her eyes flicker open.

The alarm on her clock. Her eyes adjust to the dim light. Where is she? It's her own room. Her own bed. Five o'clock. Her date with Richard.

She is awake now. She sits on the side of the bed trying to clear her mind. Yes, the nightmare is still there. Will she ever be rid of it? Will there ever be an end?

Denise Burton pulled off her clothes and climbed into the shower. Time to shake this dream. Time for reality.

He was—as she expected—prompt. Her doorbell was ringing at six-thirty and she opened it to a very goodlooking man, dressed in a blue blazer, gray pants, and a sport shirt. As usual, Richard looked great.

But Denise had had the time to dress well too, and the dark green dress she wore clung to her body, accenting her figure.

Richard was duly impressed.

"Wow. You keep looking better and better."

"Thanks, handsome. You don't look so bad yourself. I'd pick you up anytime."

He moved into the room and took her in his arms. The embrace was long and he kissed her with passion. She returned the kiss pressed against him and could feel his hand slide down her back and stroke her rear.

She pulled back. "Hey. I thought this was a dinner date."

He laughed, pulling his hands away from her in a gesture of "hands off."

"Right. That's what I promised. I did make a 7 o'clock reservation—and I think you'll find this place to your liking."

He was right.

High up on the 30th floor of a downtown hotel they sat and watched the lights of the city below. The view was spectacular.

She could see the trail of the freeway traffic, lines of white lights in one direction, red in the other, inching along the super highway. There were the tiny dots of street lights, and, on this clear evening she could see the city dramatically stretching for miles—almost to the ocean. It was a grandiose feeling, observing it all from so far above.

The food was perfect. Shrimp cocktail. Prime rib. A robust red wine. By the time they were sipping their after dinner drinks—snifters of B and B—Denise was high on the food, the drinks, and the colors shimmering beneath her.

The descending glass elevator took them down to the parking lot, and they watched as the lights became real buildings, signs, cars. His arm was around her, holding her close. Her head leaned on his shoulder. She felt protected by Richard, cared for. She wanted him to take care of her forever, to protect her from the nightmares, to hold her tightly.

As they reached the parking lot, he turned her face to his and kissed her, and she felt he cared. Maybe, just maybe, these two different people could find a life together. She felt she had found someone she might live with. But did he?

They drove quietly through the downtown streets, then onto the freeways. But this time Richard did not exit where he normally would have to take her home.

Denise noticed. "Where to now?"

"A little surprise. You've never been to my place. What d'you say?"

"Sure. I'd love to see where you live. You've been keeping it a secret from me, you know. For all I know you've got a wife and six kids waiting there."

"Not to mention the cat and dog."

"Well, I'm eager to meet them all."

But, of course, there was no family. Just a beautiful condo in Granada Hills, well furnished, comfortable, lived in.

She moved around the living room, flipped through his collection of compact discs (light classics, jazz, Beatles, Billy Joel) and was duly impressed. The books on the shelf included lots of scientific stuff plus some spy novels and piles of popular magazines. Richard had gone into the kitchen to open another bottle of wine. She felt light-headed enough but he insisted, so she agreed.

She felt agreeable to just about anything he suggested. She felt she was in love. With the moment. With the place. With Richard.

He brought the two glasses from the kitchen and handed her one. They touched the two goblets lightly.

The phone rang.

Richard picked it up but said nothing. He set the receiver down.

"I have to get this in the bedroom, Denise. I'll only be a minute."

As he closed the bedroom door behind him, she dutifully picked up the phone receiver to replace it, but as she did so, she distinctly heard the voice on the other end of the line.

"Is she there?"

And Richard: "Yes."

And the voice: "Good. Call us when you're finished."

And then the line clicked off.

Quickly she put the phone down. She was unable to understand what had just happened, but something was not right. He had told someone else she was there. There was something he was to do—to finish. She was about to sip some of the wine in her hand, but suddenly she stopped. What if— no, it couldn't be. She looked at the other glass on the table. Then she quickly exchanged the two glasses.

What kind of paranoia was this? Maybe nothing. But that call—

Richard came into the room, smiling.

"Who was it, Richard?"

"Nothing important. Just a business associate. I'll call him later."

He reached for the wine glass and they resumed their toast. They sipped the wine—Denise watching him closely. He put some music on, quietly in the background, and dimmed the lights. They sat, he with his arm around her, she with her head on his shoulder. They kissed. But she could feel him becoming more relaxed. By the time they had emptied the glasses, he was talking strangely, his words rambling—almost incoherent.

"Denise—Denise—why did you go there?"

"Go—where?"

"You shouldn't have gone out there, Denise."

"Out there?"

"To the Flats."

"Why?"

"Too deep—too deep— getting in too deep."

She watched him as he talked.

"Too deep—too deep—"

"What's on the sixth floor, Richard?"

He had fallen back on the couch, his head tipped back, his eyes closed. But still he rambled on.

"Sixth floor? God, I hate that room. Testing. Testing. Cutting. Bodies."

"Whose bodies?"

"The workers. From the Flats. Testing. Always testing."

"Was I ever up there—in the room?"

"Weeks and weeks ago. You weren't supposed to remember. The drug. Supposed to erase the memory. Damn drug must have given you the nightmares. Damn drug didn't work. Damn fucking drug."

Abruptly his head rolled over and his body went limp.

She felt his pulse, but he was still alive. This was what she would have been like if she had drunk from that glass. And what would have been her fate? To join the bodies on the ward. The bodies that were supposed to be dead but were now human experiments. Would her organs have been sliced from her and analyzed and catalogued?

The phone was ringing.

Quickly she moved into the kitchen. There on the counter was the wine bottle and beside it a small vial with powder in it.

The phone continued to ring.

She moved to the bedroom. On the dresser were some scattered items. His car keys and another ring—probably his work keys. She picked them both up. Some of them must be the keys to the rooms on the sixth floor. Could she—

The phone stopped ringing.

She moved back to where Richard's body lay inert, lying awkwardly across the couch. Quickly she searched his pockets. She found his wallet and went through the items men keep to identify themselves: credit cards, driver's license, and the one she was searching for—his Marikem ID, stamped with a top security clearance.

She had her entry now. The sixth floor room was available to her—if she dared. Kominsky had told her to stop. But she couldn't. Richard had betrayed her. She had to find out for herself. Her adrenaline was pumping. This was the Denise Burton who had taken every dare as a child; who, as a woman, had leaped from that platform held only by a bungee cord. Afraid? Yes, but she had to go back to the Marikem plant and find out what was on the sixth floor.

41 ❖
The Real Thing

SHE REMEMBERED TO TAKE his car keys, as well as the other set and his ID. There was no way for her to know how long he would be unconscious or who else might be trying to contact him. She felt sure that someone might get suspicious when there was no anwer to the phone calls. Time was precious now but there was so much to do. She had to act intelligently. She had to satisfy herself—despite the risk. She had to find out the truth.

Denise found a back stairway that went down to the alley. Richard's car was parked around the corner and she hugged the shadows of the building as she walked to it.

Then she drove quickly back to her apartment. She hoped Donald would be there but intended to head for her workplace by herself if he wasn't available.

Luckily he was there, lying on the couch watching TV.

"Donald, I don't have time to explain—I'll talk to you in the car. Please come with me."

"Where to now?"

"Marikem. I've got to find out something and this time I'll be able to get inside."

"Can you get me in too?"

"I think so. I've got Richard's ID. With any luck the guard won't notice the difference. Oh, do you still have that gun?"

"Yeah."

"Bring it. I'm not sure what we'll be getting into."

Surprised at her response, he got the weapon and they headed for the door.

But just as she was about to follow him out, she paused.

What if—what if something happened? What if there was a glitch? What if—so many things could go wrong.

Denise picked up the phone, found Kennison's number and dialed. The poor guy was probably suffering in the hospital—partially because of her—and didn't need more anguish.

But she didn't want to call Kominsky. It would be a violation of what she had promised him. At least she could leave a message—so someone would know what she was doing. Just in case something did happen.

There was the click as a message machine came on. Then the brief message. Then the beep.

"This is an important message for Rogers—from Denise Burton. I've got more information about—the story I told you about. I'm heading for the lab now—tonight. If anything happens, somebody has to get the truth out of the people in charge. Richard Kramer, at Marikem, knows a lot—if you can force him to talk. I suggest you definitely contact Marcus Kominsky at Cal Tech. Whatever is going on there is on the sixth floor. I sure hope you're feeling better."

As Denise drove, she told him what had happened at Richard's apartment. Donald's mouth fell open.

"What the hell—"

"I was surprised too—when that phone call came in. Luckily I overheard enough."

"I thought you two were pretty tight."

"Unfortunately I thought so too. It seems that all of it was just a bunch of lies. He was just leading me on—for the company. Just keeping an eye on me—but having a damn good time in the process."

She started to cry.

"Bastard—fucking bastard. I should have smashed his head in. That would've been a fair exchange for the way he treated me. If I get another chance, that's what I'll do, damn it. I'll split the bastard's skull."

"Jesus, Denise, why are we heading to Marikem? When Richard wakes up, all hell's gonna break loose, isn't it? Wouldn't it be better to head somewhere else—like Japan or Siberia—or somewhere?"

"I've got to see what's up there, that's all. Then I'll have some real evidence—to tell the press or somebody. What I have now is still just my say-so. I can't really prove much. I need to know for myself too. I've got to see that room. Are you afraid to come with me?"

"Hell, yes. But I guess I owe it to you, Denise. I'll give it a shot. Let's face it, the worst that can happen is that we both get killed."

"Thanks for your confidence."

She had dried her eyes and now was more intent on revenge than anything else. Somehow, she was thinking, she was going to make Richard Kramer pay for this. Somehow.

As they approached the Marikem guard gate, she handed Donald the ID and got hers out of her purse.

"I know he doesn't look that much like you, but act casual. Most of the time the guard hardly looks at it."

She reached the guard kiosk and both she and Donald held up their cards. The guard, a tired old employee, who was more interested in the ballgame he had playing on his portable radio, shined his flashlight into the car for an instant, then waved them through. He mumbled something about people working crazy hours and then went back into the kiosk, opening his thermos to sip some coffee.

They drove in slowly, circling the building, looking for a back entrance. Denise didn't want to take a chance on any of the night workers—if there were any in this building—seeing her.

She pulled her car up next to a side door that she recognized as the one leading to a back stairwell she had used to go down to the file room. If they could get in here, they could avoid the elevator, and anyone who might be in the building.

There was only a small light over this entrance and it was

not visible from the rest of the parking lot. If only they could get in, that was the question.

She gestured for Donald to get out and touched her finger to her lips.

She tried the door. They were in luck. It was unlocked. Quickly they moved into the building and up the stairs.

The building was ominously quiet. Just the constant hum of a generator, probably an air conditioner or something, provided the background. The stairway was dark with only a few emergency lights illuminating their way.

By the time they reached the sixth floor, they were both puffing from the exertion.

"Jesus, Denise, couldn't we use the elevator?" Donald whispered.

She shook her head and gestured for him to follow. The door at the top of the landing, however, did not respond to her attempt to open it. This was a security area. They kept things locked. Denise pulled out the key ring she had taken from Richard's dresser. Hopefully. She tried several and, at last, one worked. They were in the hallway. The sterile, white hallway. The hallway where it had all started many weeks ago. If she was correct, behind one of these doors was the answer to why she had been experiencing the frightening nightmares.

Suddenly she paused. Wait a minute. Richard had said to her—as he was slipping into unconsciousness—that she shouldn't have gone to the Flats. How did he know? Who knew she had been there? Donald, the reporter Kennison, Kominsky—and the therapist, Dr. Glidden.

Were her sessions being taped for someone else? Was every word going back to the honchos at Marikem? Jesus Christ. They were monitoring her every move. These people were insidious. Kominsky had them pegged all right. It was all something right out of "The Twilight Zone."

Denise tried to remember where she had first encountered Richard. They turned a corner to a second hallway and it all came back to her.

This was it. There—that was the door he had gone through. Was it the place she wanted? She moved to it. Donald followed. Nothing on the door indicated what was there but a number: 644. Again she took out the key ring. Yes. Again one of the keys worked.

She peered into the dim light of the room. There it all was. The image of her dreams. The hospital ward. Bodies covered with plastic sheeting. Monitoring machines whizzing and ticking. There must have been ten or fifteen beds. Each occupied by a living being. Barely living. She had been here before. The room really existed. Her mind was not deceiving her. But the people at Marikem were.

Donald stood behind her aghast. He remembered what she had told him of her dreams. And here was the proof. But what more was she intending to do?

Denise moved along the aisle past the beds. Ahead of her was the door to the surgery. She was determined to see if it, too, was real.

42 ❖
Awake

IN THE HAZE OF HIS STUPOR, Richard Kramer was aware of a thundering noise. Like crashing wood and splintering metal, the vibrations reverberated in his head. A hand was slapping his face, trying to rouse him. Then he could feel himself jerked rudely to his feet—unable to stand—but pulled by rough hands—propelled along. There was a thunderous rush in his ears, like a waterfall, and then he felt the stinging blast of water—frigid water—hit his face and cascade all over him soaking his clothing, forcing him to come out of his haze.

He stood in the shower, cold water running over his clothed body, shivering. Two men held him upright and he could see another figure standing in the bathroom. Soon the blur came into focus as he regained consciousness. The massive bulk of Otto Gesselman stood watching him. Then the other two awkwardly pulled him out of the shower and he stood shivering and dripping face to face with the huge man.

"You should get those wet things off, Richard. You don't want to catch cold."

Richard was about to start doing so, still not totally aware of what had happened, but Gesselman was no longer interested in humor.

"Where the hell is she?"

"She?"

"The woman, damn it. The Burton woman!"

"I don't know."

"What happened?"

"I—I put a tranquilizer in her drink. But—somehow—I must have been the one who drank it."

"Damn it. I knew we shouldn't have left this to you."

Richard Kramer was now aware of a throbbing in his head—a pulsating headache that forced him to sit down on the toilet seat, head in hands.

"Any ideas, Richard?"

He was trying to think. "I guess she might have gone home. Or—I don't know."

"Okay. Manny, try her place. Al, stay here till Richard gets his shit together. I'll be back at the office. Call me right away if you find out anything."

And he thundered out of the room.

Slowly Richard Kramer peeled off his soggy clothing, leaving the puddle lying on the bathroom floor. He dried himself slowly, feeling that he really needed to lie down, the pain was vibrating in his head, his whole body ached. He found his robe hanging behind the door and slipped it on over his still damp body. He moved—still somewhat unsteadily through the apartment. He noticed the man Al watching him but ignored him and continued to the bedroom. He really wanted to lie down.

As he moved into the room, he looked down at his dresser top. Something should have been there but wasn't.

"My keys! Where are my keys?"

The other man, Al, heard him and quickly moved into the room.

"What keys?"

Denise and Donald stood in the operating room in the dim light. It was all exactly the way she remembered it, but now it was deserted. The table was there, there were trays for instruments, and she even noticed a container in the corner with "Project X-29" stencilled on the side. It was all real. The nightmares were real. Somehow she had stumbled onto this room and they had tried to erase it from her memory. But they had not succeeded. They had only pushed it into her subconscious and the recurring nightmares kept reminding her of what had happened. But now she had the proof. They could not stop her now.

"I've seen enough, Donald. Let's get out of here."

"Fine with me. I hate hospitals. They scare the shit out of me."

"This place scares me too."

They moved back into the larger room and Denise looked at the bodies as she passed them. These were human beings who had now become experiments for Marikem. Nothing was wasted here. Nothing was sacred either. As far as they were concerned, these plastic sheeted creatures might just as well have been laboratory animals. For the greater good of Marikem.

"Where to now, Denise?"

"It's time to let the world know what these inhuman creeps are doing. We've got a long night ahead of us."

They moved to the hallway door. Donald opened it carefully but she noticed that it seemed even darker than when they had come in.

As they moved through it, suddenly hands were grabbing them, holding their arms, gagging their mouths, forcing them into submission. And as she felt her arms pinned behind her, one thought flashed in Denise's mind. She realized she should have listened to Professor Marcus Kominsky.

43 ❖
Claustrophobia

THE FLOOR WAS HARD where she lay. Her head was throbbing too. Wherever she was, it was pitch black. She tried to recall what had happened and forced herself to remember but all she could think of was leaving the operating room with Donald, being grabbed from behind and held, and then—and then—what? That smell. Sickening sweet. It still lingered on her face. Some kind of anesthetic. It must have been.

How long had she been here? Just where in hell was she anyway? Where was Donald?

She could hear breathing—deep breathing—nearby. Someone else was here too. And then the sound of a body rolling over. Could Donald be here too?

"Donald?" she called out tentatively.

"Who's that?" It was his voice.

"It's me—Denise. Can you see anything?"

"Hell, no. Jesus, Denise, what hit us?"

"They just put us out with something. Can't you smell it?"

"Yeah. That's what that is. Wow, do I have a headache!"

"Where do you think we are?"

"Beats the shit out of me."

"Maybe there's a door somewhere."

She could hear him pulling himself up and his stumbling footsteps moving haltingly around the room. She sat up and waited.

"Find anything?"

"Not yet."

"There's got to be a door somewhere."

Then she heard him at the far corner of the room.

"I found it. But it's locked tight. Wherever we are, we're gonna be here for a while."

"Do you think they're going to kill us?"

"Who knows. But you'd think they would have done it by now—if that was what they had in mind."

"Probably would have."

"We're just going to have to wait it out—until somebody decides what they're going to do with us."

"Just sit here in the dark, huh."

"I guess so."

"Sounds like they're trying to drive us crazy from claustrophobia."

"Maybe that's their plan."

"Whoever they are."

They sat silently on the floor. Waiting.

Rogers Kennison at that moment was sitting up in his hospital bed, holding a piece of paper in his hand. On it was the message Denise had left on his answering machine, a message that had been dutifully brought to him by his roommate, Steve. Fortunately he was feeling better. His body was sore and banged up, but he was alive and he was somewhat functional. He wondered how Gerry was doing.

He was thinking about the accident, their visit to the ghost town, the graveyard, and Denise. He looked at the note again. Now she was heading back to the lab—possibly into more danger. He picked up the phone by his bed and dialed 411. Was there a Marcus Kominsky listed in the Pasadena area? Sure enough, there was. He dialed the number they gave him and a man's voice answered.

"Is this Dr. Kominsky?"

"Yes, who's this?"

"My name is Kennison, Dr. Kominsky. I'm a reporter for the *News Telegram*."

"Sorry, I don't do interviews—on anything."

"That's not why I called. It's about a friend of yours—Denise Burton."

"What about her?"

"She talked to me a few days ago about some things that were going on out at the Marikem test facility at Frampton Flats."

"Yes."

"Well—she left a message on my machine tonight that she had found out some more information and was going back to the plant. Do you know anything about it?"

"No. Where are you now?"

Rogers hesitated, then he explained.

"I hate to admit it but I'm in a hospital bed. I was in an accident—and it may well be tied to this whole business at Marikem."

Another pause. Then Kominsky exploded.

"That crazy woman. What the hell is she trying to do? She's going to end up getting herself killed—from her own stupidity!"

"Dr. Kominsky, do you you have any more information on this whole thing?"

"I may have tomorrow."

"Well, if we don't hear from Denise Burton by then, I think it's time to confront these people and expose whatever we know of this story."

"I have to tell you, Mr. Kennison, I don't trust reporters. I've had too many bad experiences with them."

"I'm sorry to hear that, Dr. Kominsky, but this time you're just going to have to trust me. I know enough folks from the media to put some pressure on these people at Marikem—hopefully before something happens to Denise Burton. If you can provide some more facts, we may be able to get the goods on them. Please help me—and help her."

Kominsky thought for a minute.

"I'll call you in the morning. Give me your room number."

Rogers gave him the number and hung up.

44 ❖
Help from Another Source

THEY MUST HAVE SAT in the dark for more than an hour, talking quietly about many things. Neither Donald nor Denise seemed scared.

They had time so they talked. About their lives. About the past. Even about what they thought of each other. Why not be truthful? It might be their last honest conversation. Or their last conversation—of any kind.

"So you really think I'm a total loser, huh, Denise?"

"I hate to admit it, but yeah. You've screwed up your life more times than I can count. You ruined our marriage. Let's face it, Donald, I don't really see much change in the last few weeks."

"Well, you're probably right. I keep thinking about making changes, but everytime I try something, I fuck it up."

"But look at the bright side. You're not responsible for the mess we're in now. I get the credit for this one. So if we both end up dead, you can blame me. I got you into this."

"Don't worry. Whatever happens, I won't blame you. What you did took a lot of guts, and I'm glad I was with you to help out."

"Thanks, Donald. I really appreciate that. Honestly."

She could hear him sliding across the floor to where she was and then his presence close to her.

She could feel his arm reach out in the dark and hold her and it felt warm and comforting. Then she felt his hand reach up to her face, stroking and soothing and it felt good. He was a genuine comfort in this lonely limbo.

She would have had a lot of trouble enduring this alone.

Then they heard the metal sound of keys. Keys unlocking the door.

A muted shaft of light was now visible as the door squeaked open. A silhouetted figure stood in the open doorway, then moved into the room. Then a faintly familiar voice broke the silence.

"You folks okay?"

It was the old man. The old man of Frampton Flats. Varny McAvoy.

Denise and Donald both pulled themselves up, surprised. She spoke first.

"Is that you, Mr. McAvoy?"

"Yep, it's me."

"Where are we?"

"You're in a room at the test plant—at the Flats."

"Really? What—are you doing here?"

"I come over to get you out. I saw them bring the both of you in. You was out cold. When they left, I come over to get yuh."

"They didn't leave any guards?"

"Nope. They must'uh figgered you was locked up good and tight. They didn't expect me to help yuh."

"How did you get in?"

"Oh, I got me a master key. Part o'my job's keepin' an eye on this place."

"I don't know how to thank you."

"No thanks needed. Come on, let's git goin'."

They moved out of the room, down the long, empty halls of the test facility she had only recently tried to break into. There wasn't much to see—even if you could see much in the dim light. It was just a massive, deserted building.

They followed McAvoy through the maze of corridors to a stairwell and then down the reverberating metal stairs to a doorway. Then out into the night. The chill desert air made Denise shiver as they trudged across the sand down the long path until they reached the fence and gate where they had first encountered this man in the flannel shirt and jeans. He unlocked the gate (he seemed to have all the keys they needed) and they continued after him down the road to his tiny shelter.

As they walked, Denise realized they had no car, and McAvoy didn't have one either. Somehow they had to get back to the city. Somehow they had to get a car.

Just as they reached his tiny shack, they heard it. The sound of a car approaching—fast. Quickly they ducked into McAvoy's little house and watched as a large, black Mercury roared up to the gate and a man got out from the passenger side, unlocked it, got back in and the car moved up to the plant.

They had to get moving. Perhaps hide in the town. They left the house and headed down the road.

But in minutes another car was roaring up the road and pulled to a stop directly in front of them. It was a shiny, red Camaro. A single figure got out and Denise recognized the figure immediately. It was Richard Kramer.

They stood there in the glare of the headlamps: Denise, McAvoy, Donald—and Richard Kramer. It was as if the moment was frozen, as if no one knew exactly what to do. Here stood the man she had thought was her friend and lover and now she knew him as her enemy. Should she run? Attack him? Tell Donald to lunge at him? But she did nothing—too stunned by his appearance, too surprised to see him standing there in front of her.

Richard spoke first.

"Denise, I need to talk to you. Now. Alone."

"I don't think we have anything to say to each other, Richard. You should just be thankful I don't have a weapon or I'd damn well use it on you. Without thinking twice."

"You've got me all wrong, Denise. Believe me."

"I don't think so, Richard. Tell me the truth. In my dream—in the operating room. That really was you. You were there, weren't you?"

"Yes."

"All this time you've been seeing me just to keep an eye on me—for the fucking company. For your goddamned bosses."

"That's true, but—"

"No buts, Richard. You're a sneaking bastard. Everything we've shared has been phony."

"No, Denise. That's where you're wrong. It's all been genuine. I swear it. Please, just come here for a minute. They can watch from where they are. I just want a few words with you—alone."

She turned to Donald and McAvoy. Donald shrugged, then suggested, "I can watch from here, Denise. Give the guy a minute."

McAvoy said nothing, but cradled his shotgun in his arms.

She followed Richard to the back of the car out of the white glare of the headlamps. She noticed the very sporty red Z-28. He must have borrowed it from somebody since she had taken his car. Richard paused and leaned against the rear fender but did not look at her.

"What I'm going to tell you, Denise, you're going to have to believe—to accept on faith. I can prove it later on, but for now you must believe me."

"Go ahead. I'll decide when I hear it."

"I don't just work for Marikem. I also work for a federal agency—UAD—Undercover Analysis Division. We're part of an overseeing group that monitors federal contract holders. For the past three years I've been at Marikem as an undercover agent checking every aspect of the company's operations. Unfortunately when you stumbled onto that room on the sixth floor, I was all set to prepare my report on them—to blow the whole operation. But once you showed up, I had to follow through on their plan to keep you quiet. At the same time they were experimenting with the drug they shot you with to see if it would work removing the memory of what you saw. If that had happened, I could have finished my analysis of them and indicted the boss and half the bigwigs there. But once the nightmares started hitting you, I had to follow up on what they wanted me to do."

"And I suppose if they had said to kill me, you would have done that too?"

"Never. I love you, Denise. I wouldn't hurt you."

"Sure. And the junk you put in the wine?"

"Just a mild tranquilizer."

"And if I had swallowed it?"

"I had intended to have you taken to a safe house we run and then publish my report."

"But you could have just told me this at your place that night."

"I couldn't. I thought the place was being watched. You had to leave there in a drugged state. Then I would have told you."

"I still don't believe you, Richard. You've lied to me too many times now and for all I know this might be another one."

"I know, but I can prove all this. And there's something else. The chemist—Stuart Neal—who killed himself. It may very well not have been suicide. These people have to be stopped."

She looked at him. What was the truth? How could she be sure?

Suddenly they heard Donald's voice.

"Denise, that car's coming back."

In the distance they could see the headlamps coming down the road from the plant.

45
Missing Person

Marcus Kominsky was sleeping badly. As a matter of fact, he wasn't sleeping much at all. He tossed and turned with recurring images of Denise Burton in his head. Aspects of her story kept recurring—the nightmares, the graveyard at Frampton Flats, and he kept seeing her in dire straits—or worse yet—her body being carted out to a spot in the cemetery with the others.

He looked at his clock radio. The digital red glow told him it was 3:18 in the morning. He pulled himself up and picked up the phone by the bedside. What the hell. It's for her own good. If she's there, I'll be relieved. If she isn't, what then? I'll worry about that when the time comes.

But she was not there. Her machine answered and he left a message for her. Unless she could sleep though a ringing phone—or had the ringer off, of course. But he was worried and pulled himself up trying to figure out where she might be. Then he got dressed.

She could see the other car approaching and she knew they had to act quickly. At the moment, Richard seemed her only hope. If he was telling the truth, he could help them. If not, things were no worse than if the other car caught them here. She decided to take the one chance open to them.

"Okay, Richard. Get us out of here."

They scrambled into the Camaro with Donald in the back seat.

McAvoy stood quietly by the door of his little home.

"You folks be careful, y'hear," was his only comment.

"Thanks, Mr. McAvoy. You've been great."

"No problem. But you'd better git movin'."

Richard executed a rapid U-turn and the sleek car, billowing dust in its wake, took off.

By the time they had gone through the deserted town and started back on the narrow highway leaving Frampton Flats, Donald, checking out the back window, could see lights about a mile back.

"We better make tracks. I think that Mercury has decided to come after us."

Richard checked the rear view. "You're right. I think we may have to see how well this little machine can operate. Buckle up tight, folks."

He hit the accelerator hard and the Camaro took off shooting ahead and reaching 85 with no effort at all. Behind them the Mercury was doing likewise and they knew they were in for a battle of the engines.

Rogers Kennison was also sleeping badly. He tossed and turned in his hospital bed, the aches and bruises annoying him more this night than they had after the initial accident. He was worried. He had tried to reach Denise before he went to sleep—or tried to go to sleep—and had gotten nothing but her answering machine. He felt somewhat responsible, but lying here made him feel rather useless. His watch showed him it was almost four in the morning. He wondered what he could do.

He struggled out of bed, aching in every muscle, and went to the closet where his clothing hung. He fished in his pants pocket and pulled out the tiny address book he always kept. He knew most of the important media people in town and they would probably listen to him if he got on the phone and called them at their homes. If he could pressure Marikem to come up with some answers—to reveal what was going on on the sixth floor—by getting a bunch of media people there, they might have one hell of a story. Most important of all, somebody needed to ask them just where Denise Burton was. He sat on the side of the bed and started marking the book, marking the names of those he felt sure would listen to him and go to Marikem's offices that morning. He also wondered if he could get himself dressed, get Steve over there early, and be part of the entourage that arrived. After all, it was his story. He didn't want to miss the action.

46
Pursuit of Happiness

THE SPEEDOMETER ON THE Z-28 read 95 as the car careened through the desert over the bumpy road. Luckily it handled well and Richard maneuvered it skillfully. Behind them the Mercury kept pace, trying to close the distance, but not succeeding. Every time it started to move closer, Richard accelerated and the obliging V-8 engine responded, moving ahead of their pursuer.

Soon they were on the highway, and in minutes were approaching the freeway. Richard pulled the car onto the ramp and headed back toward the city. All of them breathed a collective sigh of relief to be heading back over a smooth superhighway. But the Mercury did not give up its chase. It stayed behind them, still trying to overtake their car but finding it a difficult task. Richard had hoped to lose their pursuers by maneuvering among the other cars, but there was virtually no one else on the road at this hour and their sporty red vehicle was no problem to keep in view. He was still keeping the speed at over 90 and the few other cars on the road kept well out of the way of this crazy driver zooming through the darkness at breakneck velocity.

Denise, the practical one, spoke first. "Richard, what about the cops?"

"Good point. Sooner or later somebody's going to spot one of us. Let's hope they see the guys behind us first."

And their luck held. Just as they roared by an exit ramp and the Mercury did the same, a Highway Patrol car pulled on, spotted the speeding black vehicle, and, lights flashing, forced it over to face the music.

Immediately Richard slowed to a manageable 70—which seemed like slow motion after what they had been going through—and they were—at least for now—home free.

"Well, we got lucky this time. What do we do now?" was Donald's comment from the rear as he stared out the back window.

"We can't go back to Denise's place—or mine. I think we should get a hotel room somewhere in the valley and you two can stay there until I get back to make my report. Getting the Marikem people out of commission may take a few days so you two should be somewhere safe."

Denise looked at Richard. Maybe—at last—he was telling the truth. He had gotten them out safely and seemed to be intent on keeping them that way. She began to realize how difficult it must have been for him to live such a complicated double life.

"If you really have the clout you say you have, Richard, how about getting us a police guard or something. These people mean business and we may not be so lucky the next time."

"I'll see if I can. I can probably get someone from my office to keep an eye on you until the dust clears."

"That sure would be appreciated."

They sped back to the city as the streaks of daylight began to appear in the sky. It was the lovely rose colored glow of dawn but none of them felt in much of a mood to enjoy it. They were all tired, especially Denise and Donald. A hotel bed and a shower seemed like a good idea.

But this day was just beginning for them. Little did any of them know just how eventful a day it would be.

By 8:30, Kennison had made several calls to media friends and piqued their interest enough to guarantee their appearance at Marikem's offices that morning. He figured ten would be a good time to meet there, but decided that warning the Marikem bigwigs in advance was not a good idea. The element of surprise was important.

By nine his friend Steve had arrived, and ignoring the protests of the nurses, got him dressed and ready to check out.

As they struggled to get his shoes and socks on, the phone rang. It was Kominsky. Unfortunately he had no more information to supply, but when Rogers told him about the media assault they had planned for the morning, he agreed to show up in spite of his normal aversion to reporters. He promised to be there primarily as an observer.

But unfortunately there was to be no surprise. Meredith Mathison had been called from the Mercury as it pursued Richard's car through the early hours of the morning, and called once again after the humiliation of the traffic ticket. By seven he had put his damage control program into effect, and when the phone rang in his office at nine, he was prepared. A friend in the media informed him that reporters were on their way to the plant and, now confident all was under control, Mathison sat back ready for any eventuality.

Kennison was preparing to leave his room with a good deal of effort; Steve was in process of helping him to the door and they were trying to decide if they should get a wheelchair to facilitate his exit with minimum pain. Again the phone rang. Steve picked it up, and he instantly handed the phone to Rogers.

Kennison's face lit up when he heard the voice.

"Jesus, Denise, where have you been all night. I've been worried sick about you."

"It's a long story. I'm in a safe place now, but it was a real close call."

"Listen, there's going to be a bit of a showdown at the OK Corral this morning. At Marikem. I'm headed there now.

We're going to confront their management with the facts we have."

"I don't know if that's a good idea right now."

"Well, it's too late to stop it. The media people are already headed there. How about you?"

"I'm exhausted, but—-all right. What time?"

"It's called for ten and I hope it'll be a surprise for their management."

"I doubt that. They seem to know almost everything that's going on."

"We'll see."

"Say, are you back in one piece yet?"

"Barely. But I don't want to miss this."

"We'll see you there."

Denise turned to Richard and Donald as she hung up.

"It's hit the fan. Kennison has a whole slew of reporters heading for Marikem this morning. They're going to confront the bigwigs and force some answers out of them."

Richard was furious. "They can't. They've got to stop this. It'll ruin everything I've been preparing and we'll never get them."

"It's too late, Richard."

"Dammit. Look, you two stay here. I'm heading for the office. I've got to do something or this whole thing—all I've been working on for over a year now—may be destroyed. Get some rest. I'll keep you informed."

He rushed out of the room.

Denise looked at Donald.

"He wants us to stay here. And all hell may be about to break loose at Marikem."

"You also happen to be the best witness they have, Denise."

"Right."

"Do you think we can rent a car without too much hassle?"

"My credit's still good. Even if yours may not be, Donald."

"Do you think you can stay awake?"

"No problem in that department. Want to get cleaned up?"

She looked at the clock by the bedside.

"It's after nine, Donald. I think we should skip the niceties and get our tails over there."

"I agree. This may be the bomb that blows the whole thing sky high."

"Maybe, Donald. But the Marikem people are shrewd as hell. I wouldn't put anything past them at this point."

"Maybe, but I sure as hell want to see what happens."

"Say, how are we going to get into that place. My ID's probably worth very little at this point."

Donald took out his wallet and pulled out some cards. "Do you think this might have some clout?"

He was holding a press card and it looked very official.

"Jesus, where'd you get that?"

"Let's just say I collect little items like this—from my various travels."

"Looks good to me. Let's give it a try."

"Okay. First, however, I think we should come up with a vehicle."

Quickly they headed down to the hotel lobby to find a car to rent.

In the lobby of Fuller Memorial Hospital, Rogers sat impatiently waiting as Steve negotiated with the administration for his release. It was difficult, but Steve's calm, patient reassurance that he would bring the injured man back in a few hours finally got through. Rogers watched as he signed papers with the chief administrator looking on unhappily. Then he noticed a familiar figure entering the building. It was Rhonda Gotschalk.

"Rhonda!"

She saw him and quickly approached the wheelchair.

"God, Rogers, you don't look in any condition to be released."

"Well, it's just a temporary release. How's Gerry doing?"

"Better. There are broken ribs. And his face is a real mess. But they say the concussion is minor and he's breathin' okay so his lungs are workin' all right, but I'm sure it hurts. I think he's gonna make it."

"That's good news."

Steve was now behind him. Rogers looked up at the clock on the lobby wall.

"We've got to make tracks, Rhonda. It's sure good seeing you and hearing about Gerry."

"Take it easy, will yuh. I'll tell Gerry you were askin' about him."

Steve quickly moved the wheelchair toward the door as Rogers waved to Gerry's wife.

47 ❖
Power of the Press

THE AUDITORIUM OF THE Marikem facility was a well designed theater used for various meetings, press conferences,
and symposia. There were about a hundred upholstered ma-
roon theater seats, a small stage with a lectern (complete with
a dramatic logo and "Marikem Industries" etched on the
front in a contemporary typeface), and there was a screen that
could descend at the flick of a switch. At the back, space was
set aside for the TV camera people to set up their tripods and
equipment. By ten there were four TV crews assembling
their electronic gear and about twenty of the seats down front
were occupied with reporters from the print media and the
field people from the various television stations.

Rogers Kennison had arrived dramatically, pushed in the
wheelchair Steve had commandeered from the hospital. It
was now placed strategically in the aisle close to the stage.

When they had arrived at the gate, Kennison was surprised that the whole thing had been so easy—almost as if all
was ready for the press onslaught. The guard had let them in
and directed them to a press rep who pointed out the location
of the auditorium. "So much for the element of surprise," he
thought as they joined the other press cars parked outside the
meeting room.

Inside, Kennison talked to several of those he knew—
some he didn't know—but they had apparently gotten the
word from somewhere, just as—apparently—the powers of
Marikem had.

Soon the assembled press had settled in, the cameras
were ready, and a young woman stepped up to the lectern.

"Good morning, ladies and gentlemen. My name is Virginia Latham and I'm Director of Public Affairs here at Marikem. Apparently someone has informed you there was a story to report here today—even though we did not issue a media advisory, so we are a bit surprised why you're all here.

"However, Mr. Mathison, our Chief Executive Officer, has consented to interrupt his busy schedule to answer any questions you might have about our facility and, perhaps, put to rest any rumors or false information that may have been circulating about our projects and what exactly goes on here at Marikem. Mr. Mathison."

Mathison made his dramatic entrance, striding across the stage to the lectern. He was impeccably dressed in a gray suit with a striped red and blue tie and a handkerchief peeping out from his breast pocket. His grey hair was neatly combed and he looked as if he had carefully prepared for this appearance. He exuded confidence as he stood in front of the assembled media.

"Good morning. I'm Meredith Mathison and I'm happy to see members of the press interested in what we're doing here at Marikem. One thing about our facility is its accessibility—we welcome scrutiny from anyone—especially you folks—at any time.

"Of course, we are involved in a number of government projects that are classified but—unless the government says it's off limits, you're welcome to inspect any of our labs, test facilities, or what you will."

He paused dramatically.

Herb Edelman, rose quickly to his feet, anticipating Mathison's request for any questions. He was a reporter for a local paper that specialized in exposés and he was dressed in his usual worn brown suit. He was in his fifties and had been around newspapers for many years working for some of the best ones all over the country. But he had a drinking problem and now was relegated to this modest local after many years of being with the big guys.

"Mr. Mathison, we've heard about a certain Project X-29, and we want more information about it."

"Well, some of that is classified, but I can tell you it has to do with developing some chemicals for military use. We've been working on it for several years now."

"Are these poison gases?"

"Hardly. You may not be aware, but poison gases are totally outlawed by international treaty. These are products that can provide cover for ground forces but are hardly lethal. I can't say much more than that about them."

Kennison pulled himself to his feet (with considerable effort) and called out, "Mr. Mathison, what exactly happened last year at Frampton Flats and how does this tie in with your Project X-29?"

"We have a test facility at Frampton Flats—out in the desert. We had a number of projects going on out there—including the one called X-29. As many of you know, there was an unfortunate accident that occurred last year and we have since closed down the facility."

Kennison was still on his feet, hanging on to the back of the chair, "How many people died at Frampton Flats?"

"There were no fatalities at the time of the accident, but there have been a few subsequent deaths. This is indeed a terrible tragedy, but sometimes things can happen at any test facility."

"How many fatalities, Mr. Mathison?"

"I don't have the exact figures in front of me, but I can get them for you."

"That won't be necessary, sir. I've been there and seen all the graves. There must be at least fifty."

There was an audible reaction from those in the room.

"I don't believe your information is correct."

Kennison wasn't finished. "Mr. Mathison, what's on the sixth floor of this facility—room 644 to be exact?"

"Just an experimental lab, like those on other floors."

"Can we have access to it—today?"

"Absolutely. We'll be happy to conduct a tour for you as soon as all your questions have been answered."

From the back of the room, a new voice was heard.

"I doubt if you'll see what I saw in that room yesterday."

Denise and Donald Burton stood there and the TV cameras quickly panned to where they stood, sensing a dramatic moment, something guaranteed to be featured on the evening news.

Mathison had his glasses on and was trying to ascertain who the speaker was.

"Young lady, may I ask just who you are?"

"Yes. My name is Denise Burton and I work for this company. I saw live bodies on the sixth floor last evening—live bodies your people were experimenting on—just like animals."

She moved down the aisle followed by Donald and the cameras stayed on her as she reached the edge of the stage and stood confronting Mathison.

"Mr. Mathison, I was up there last night and saw it all. Then your goons grabbed us, drugged us, and locked us up out at Frampton Flats."

Mathison did not lose his composure. He remained supremely in control. He knew exactly how to handle this hysterical woman without descending to her level. He was in charge and he intended to stay in charge.

"Miss—uh—Burton is it?"

"Yes."

"You have a very vivid imagination, Miss Burton. I'm sure your story will make very good copy for the tabloids, but there isn't a shred of evidence that it has any validity."

Donald quickly spoke up.

"Well, then I must have a vivid imagination also, because I saw exactly what she saw."

"And who are you?"

"I'm her husband—her ex-husband, that is. I was with

her last night when she went up there. And I might also add that your guys grabbed me too."

Mathison remained cool and totally controlled.

"Apparently you both can prove these allegations, I suppose. But the story seems rather fantastic to me. You easily gained access to a security area, were kidnapped—so you say—and miraculously got away just in time to be present here."

Another man had appeared on the stage and was whispering in Mathison's ear. He placed a file folder on the lectern in front of the CEO.

Denise was not about to be easily silenced.

"I can produce witnesses to the fact that we were locked up last night in your Frampton Flats plant as well as someone who helped us get away from there. I can describe in detail exactly what I saw on the sixth floor, and I can also produce a witness who knows all about the accident at Frampton Flats."

Mathison cut in.

"Miss Burton, I have an evaluation of your work performance in front of me and it does not seem favorable at all.

"There is even reference to fantastic stories you constantly tell your co-workers—and swear to be true. I also see you requested to see a therapist and have been having psychological counseling for some weeks now. This report also shows somewhat erratic attendance and work habits on the job. It indicates you have been absent for the last two days specifically—without contacting your supervisor. I personally find no credibility in your story. But I leave that all to the press to decide."

Kennison had remained on his feet, shakey but unwilling to give up—even though Mathison seemed to have the reporters on his side.

"I think we all want that tour of your sixth floor lab, Mr. Mathison—and right now might be an appropriate time."

"Certainly. Just follow me."

He moved from the stage as the reporters quickly followed.

The camera people busily released their cameras from the tripods, and, hoisting them on their shoulders, jockeyed for position as they followed the others down the aisle. Soon they were jammed into an elevator—at least most of them. The less aggressive ones were forced to follow on a second elevator and Denise and Donald found themselves in this second group. But no one threw questions at Denise as they rode up the six flights. The group of photographers remained quiet and it was a rather staid group that ascended to the security floor.

To Denise it seemed that this was an assemblage more interested in the visual than in the word, and, alone with two people they had eagerly focused their equipment on just minutes ago, they were now unable to think of anything to ask.

As the doors opened, Denise found herself for the third time (that she remembered) in the hallway with the stark white walls. The first group stood waiting, and Mathison, standing slightly apart from the reporters, immediately confronted his employee.

"Now, Miss Burton, since you claim you were here last night, perhaps you'd do us the honor of leading the way."

Denise followed by Donald, then the rest of the entourage, moved directly to the room she and Donald had visited the night before, and she pointed to the door.

"This is the room."

Smiling, Mathison opened the door and the group eagerly rushed in.

Richard Kramer paced outside his supervisor's door. He kept looking at his watch and wondering what was happening at the plant. They had to move now with their subpoenas but red tape was holding things up. All of his hard work—for a solid year—might vanish and leave them with nothing, and all because of some eager reporters and the inexorably slow wheels of the bureaucracy.

Finally he was called in and he faced his chief. Arnold Marky was a man in his 60's with a neatly trimmed beard and graying hair who always dressed immaculately. He was wearing a blue suit with a bright red tie looking as if he'd only that moment showered and dressed even though he had been at his desk for over three hours.

"What's the word, Arnold?"

"We're waiting to clear the paperwork, Richard. I just got a call and it'll be a little while longer."

"Arnold, don't you understand. We can't wait. The press is at Marikem right this minute—and if they don't have much evidence, it'll all be laughed at. I know Mathison. He's a smooth operator. By this time, he may already have them all in the palm of his hand."

"So what? The real story will come out when we serve the subpoenas. No matter when that is."

"But don't you see, he's going to be covering his ass right and left now. We've got to move."

"We can't do anything yet, Richard. Be patient."

And Richard dropped into a leather chair, fuming and frustrated.

Now the media was filing into the large room on the sixth floor, following Denise and Donald and Mathison. But the room no longer resembled the room of her nightmares. Instead of patients in hospital beds, there were row upon row of animal cages, inhabited by white rats and rabbits. White jacketed technicians moved about with clipboards, jotting down notes and recording data from screens that monitored information about each cage.

Denise stood for a moment dumbfounded. She knew that Marikem was good at damage control but this rapid transformation even had her confused. She looked around. Maybe she was wrong about the room she had chosen. She was bleary-eyed from lack of sleep and maybe she was confused. Then she saw the door at the far end of the room—the door to the surgery. This was the right place—but they had transformed it. Quickly she moved to the end of the room. One of the white jacketed technicians tried to stop her, but she pushed by him and approached the door. She could hear the others following. She pulled it open, not knowing exactly what to expect.

It was the surgery room she remembered, but the patient on the table that lay anesthetized and surrounded by gowned observers was hardly a human. A white rabbit lay asleep with a deep incision in its underside. The surgeons turned to the interlopers, annoyed at the intrusion and the group sheepishly retreated back to the large room.

No one knew quite what to do. Should they question Denise? Or Mathison? What was there to say? Had they all come here on some bizarre wild goose chase?

Denise looked at the assembled press people.

"You've got to believe me. They changed this room. There were real people in here last night—not animals. And in that surgery room I know they cut up people—experimented with them."

The cameramen had not turned on their equipment. The reporters' pens and tape recorders remained in their pockets. There was nothing they could prove now—it was all just Denise's and Donald's stories, and they seemed just too far-fetched.

Mathison turned to the group, "Are there any questions, ladies and gentlemen?"

Even Rogers Kennison who had come up in the wheelchair was not sure what to do, but he made a try, "What about the Frampton Flats facility?"

"We can give you a tour there too if you wish," replied Mathison. "But there is nothing to see. It's just an empty plant. Anything else?"

"What about the graves?"

"People die wherever you are. We provided a cemetery for our town. Is that so unusual?"

The others said nothing.

"If you have anything further, I can always be reached. Thank you all for your interest."

Mathison strode confidently to the door.

The group moved quietly to the elevators.

Denise stood with Donald, watching. Kennison sat quietly in the wheelhair, Steve behind him. There was another figure in the room that Denise had not even noticed before. Marcus Kominsky was there, hovering in the background, quietly watching. He moved to where she stood. She was exhausted, annoyed, frustrated, ready to cry.

"As you see, Miss Burton, Meredith Mathison is very resourceful. That has always been one of his trademarks."

"They've made me look like a fool, haven't they?" muttered Denise.

"Perhaps. But I'm not sure the game is totally over," suggested Kominsky.

Kennison was still on her side. "I'm not finished with this story, Denise. I've been out there and I believe what you're saying."

Kominsky moved to the door. "For now, however, I think we should call it a day."

They rode down silently to the main lobby and crossed to the large glass doors at the main entrance to the plant. As Marcus Kominsky followed them, he heard a voice behind him.

"Ah, Marcus. I didn't realize you were here."

Behind him stood Meredith Mathison, smiling and confident.

"Nice to have you back, Marcus. It's been a long time."

"Yes, Meredith, it has been a while. I just dropped by to see what the press was so concerned about."

"And you see it was all nothing. You know we operate totally aboveboard here, Marcus. There's too much at stake to do otherwise."

"There are those who might not totally agree with that, Meredith."

"Well, there are always critics. Any interest in coming back to join us some time, Marcus? We can always use a good research chemist."

"I don't think so. I'm enjoying what I do too much. Teaching may not pay as well, but at least I have no trouble sleeping nights."

Mathison smiled.

Denise, Donald, Kennison and Steve were outside the building now. They could see the reporters getting into their cars and the television crews packing the gear into their mini-vans.

But suddenly they noticed four cars moving quickly across the parking lot clearly marked on the sides with the emblem of the U.S. Federal Marshal's Office. In an instant they had pulled up next to the building and a large group of official-looking figures were invading the headquarters of Marikem Industries.

Something was about to happen. The media people could smell it. They leaped out of their vehicles, grabbing their equipment, and ran back to the building to get the story that was about to break. Denise and Donald with Kennison and Steve eagerly followed.

48 ❖
A Familiar Face

THE MEN AND WOMEN from the Marshal's Office seemed to be all over the building. They had subpoenas for documents and files and were moving rapidly into offices and labs—sure of their destinations and exactly what they were after.

Richard Kramer with two other men stood in the lobby confronting Meredith Mathison. One of the men was speaking.

". . . as Federal Marshals, Mr. Mathison, we are serving you with an arrest warrant. The list of charges is on the affidavit I have just presented you with, and they include violation of government contract regulations, falsification of records, and fourteen other charges."

The cameras were on now and the press was crowding around, jockeying for position.

"This is ridiculous!" Mathison exploded.

"Hardly," Richard cut in. He turned to the reporters. "I've been an employee at this plant for three years and I can substantiate most of the charges. I've also been an agent for the U.S. Government—UAD—Undercover Analysis Division."

"This man is a fraud," sputtered Mathison. "Nothing he says is true."

But the reporters were now hot on the chase and the cameras were recording every word. Questions were being shouted at Richard, the marshals and Mathison in the crowded lobby and general pandemonium was ensuing.

"Is everything that Mrs. Burton's been saying true? What were the violations of the contracts? Are there really bodies somewhere in the building? Where are they? Do you have any statement, Mr. Mathison?"

The two Marshals escorted Mathison out of the building and Richard pushed through the mass of reporters to where Denise and Donald stood.

"Your timing—as usual—was perfect," she said.

"You'd be surprised how hard it was to rush this, but it seemed necessary under the circumstances so I did it. But the wheels of the government move slowly—very slowly."

Kennison turned in his wheelchair at the door and rolled up to Richard.

"Hey, I want an exclusive interview with you. I'm the one who got all this moving—"

"The one who almost blew my whole investigation."

"Well, reporters need to get the facts."

"And I'm sure you will, but right now, I've got work to do."

Richard hugged Denise, gave a quick "I'll call you," and was off to the elevator.

Kennison was watching and realizing—from the embrace—that there was more to this story—perhaps lots more than he knew.

"Who is this guy? Come on, Denise. Who is he?"

"Just a friend," she said. "Just a very good friend."

Marcus Kominsky watched the unfolding drama with a smile.

"It seems that it wasn't over after all."

"As usual, Dr. Kominsky, you were right."

"Well, your knight on the white horse seems to have arrived just at the appropriate moment."

"I would say so. And lucky for me. Oh—Dr. Kominsky—this is Donald, my ex-husband. He's been suffering through a lot of this with me over the last few days. He deserves some of the credit too."

"A pleasure, Mr. Burton. I'm glad it worked out safely for your sake as well."

"It was a bit hairy there for a time, but enough people were on our side. That sure helped a lot."

"Yes, having friends can make a major difference."

Denise looked around at the chaos now going on throughout the building.

"Well, I seem to have investigated myself out of a job—and maybe about a thousand other people too."

Kominsky was reassuring. "Don't worry. I'm sure the facility will survive. There are still enough good people to run it. And I'm sure they'll be very careful of what they do from now on. At least for a while. As for Mr. Mathison, well, he may have an interesting trial ahead of him and a lot to account for. But he's a powerful man, and I'll be curious to see how that plays out."

"I have to thank you for all you did, Dr. Kominsky—even though I didn't follow your advice—as I probably should have."

"As I believe I said once before, 20-20 hindsight is a skill we all have. Remember, my advice isn't always the best. Others have told me that in no uncertain terms. But it all worked out and I'm happy to see you alive and well."

"But exhausted. What we both need now is some sleep. It's been one hell of a day—and night."

"Then you should head home and rest. You might also disconnect your phone. Otherwise you'll have the press calling you all day long."

"Good advice again. Thanks."

She grasped his hand, and she and Donald headed out of the building.

49 ❖
Celebrity

HER AUNT VANESSA was sittting up in bed, newspapers scattered across her lap, as Denise came into the room.

"Well, hello, Miss Celebrity. You seem to be all over the papers—and the TV—these days. Congratulations."

"Thanks, Vanessa. But it's not as exciting as you might think. I seem to have lost any privacy. They're after me everywhere and I even have an offer for a book and a TV movie of the week. Can you believe it?"

"Sure. You're gonna take them, I hope."

"I don't think so."

"Are you crazy? Think of the money."

"I have. But there's another offer I'm thinking more seriously about."

"Oh—I get it—Richard."

"That's it. A little proposal of marriage."

"Ah. Now that's one you shouldn't think too long about."

"There's a problem with that one too. He's a federal agent. If I marry him, I'll probably be moving around a lot of the time—or if I don't, he'll be away for long periods."

"Oh, come on, Denise, that doesn't seem to interfere with other people's lives. Hell, they manage to work around it."

"You're probably right. And he's become rather insistent."

"Go for it, kid. I don't think you have much of a career ahead at Marikem."

"You're right there."

"And Donald?"

"Oh, I'm not worried about him. He and Rogers Kennison have already agreed to do a book together on the whole Marikem thing and I promised to supply any information I can. I think Donald may finally have something to work at—and, who knows, maybe being a writer is just the thing for him. I always thought he had enough sleazy connections to write crime novels. This may be the incentive he needs."

"Sounds almost too good to be true. Say, what about that other fellow that was hurt?"

"The photographer. They tell me he's out of the I.C. unit. It looks as if he's gonna pull through okay. There's also going to be an investigation into the death of that chemist they thought committed suicide."

"Wow. This gets more interesting by the minute."

"How are you feeling, Vanessa? Honestly."

"Pretty much the same. It's hard not being able to get around much, but this is a good place and the people are caring. I get—almost—all I need. Any nightmares recently?"

"No, surprisingly enough. Richard says the drug they gave me should eventually wear off. So maybe that's finally over."

"And how about that charming psychologist—who seems to have turned out to be a super rat fink?"

"I went by there yesterday and he seems to have moved out. I guess he was afraid he might be implicated in the whole business, so he ran for his life."

"Serves the bastard right. Well, I definitely want you to invite me to the wedding, Denise. Even if I have to be carried, I intend to be there. Understand?"

"It's a deal, Vanessa."

"So now I want you to sit down for a few minutes and tell me about the events the papers left out. I know there's lots more to it and I want to hear all the juicy details."

"Well, maybe we should save that for another time."

"How come?"

"I think you have another visitor."

In the doorway stood the imposing figure of Professor Marcus Kominsky, a bunch of flowers in one hand, a wrapped parcel in the other.

"God Almighty! What the devil brings you here, Marcus?"

"Oh, just happened to be in the neighborhood. Isn't that what I'm supposed to say?"

"You never were good at lying."

"That happens to be one of my strong points, remember?"

"I sure do. Come on over, Marcus. Let's get caught up on a few hundred years of our lives."

As he moved to the bed, Denise waved, winked at her aunt and headed for the door. As she moved off down the hall, she could hear the booming laughter of Kominsky and the voice of Vanessa, animated and happier than she had heard her in many months.

A wind was picking up in the desert. The yucca and cactus moved almost imperceptibly in the hot breeze. Varny McAvoy trudged up the slope carrying some quail he had shot and anticipated cooking for his dinner. It was about four in the afternoon and Frampton Flats—after an initial onslaught of agents and reporters—had settled down to the peace and quiet he cherished. He expected it would be like this for some time and he could enjoy the solitude and the beauty of this environment he loved so much.

But as he reached the town, he could see a car approaching and it surprised him as it pulled up to his house. There was only one person in it and he recognized her immediately.

Denise stood by the car as he approached.

"Hi, Miss Burton."

"Hi, Mr. McAvoy. Good to see you again."

"Same here."

"I came by to thank you—for all you did for me."

"It weren't much. I jest did what I felt was right."

"Well, for me it was important. You really saved my life and I'll always be grateful to you for it."

"My pleasure."

"Richard and I are going to be married—in a few months. Would you like to be there?"

"Mebbe. Jest let me know when and where."

"I sure will."

He looked down at the quail he held hanging at his side.

"Like to come in for dinner? This'll feed two easy enough."

"I'd really like to but I've got to be back in the city in an hour. Maybe next time."

"Sure."

"Are you planning to stay out here?"

"Sure thing. It's m'home. I like it here."

"Okay if I—we—come and visit now and then?"

"Love t'have you. I like the quiet—but now and again visitors is okay too."

"Good. You can expect us now and then. See you, Mr. McAvoy."

"Bye."

She got into her car, waved to him, and headed home.

Varny watched her go for a few minutes. She's a nice lady, he thought, to come all the way out here just to say thanks. Not too many folks would do that.

Then, as the car was no longer in view, he moved into his little house. There was quail to cook and dinner to prepare.

Out here there was always lots to do.

About the Author

Gerald A. Schiller has combined the two careers of classroom teaching and film making for over thirty years. In addition to being a distinguished instructor of high school English and cinema classes, he has written and/or directed more than thirty educational, documentary, and promotional films and video productions.

Many of these have earned major recognition, and he has received awards from the American Film Festival, Columbus Film Festival, Golden Gate Film Festival, and CINE (The Council on International Non-Theatrical Events).

Since retiring from teaching, Mr. Schiller has authored articles and reviews for many publications including the *Los Angeles Times*, *Sightlines*, and *Film News*. He is currently the editor of the newsletter *Multimedia News*.

Deadly Dreams is his first novel.

Although he continues to write and direct educational and documentary productions, a second mystery novel, a children's book, and a non-fiction work about the movies are currently growing inside his computer.

Mr. Schiller has two grown children and lives with his wife in Southern California.

DEATH UNDERGROUND
by Gerald A. Schiller

In the haze of the early morning, as he rolled over, Rogers Kennison knew he had a strong need to get to the bathroom. He tried to focus on the clock by the bedside and thought the red numbers indicated 6:25. Too early to get up. But there was that nagging need to empty his swollen bladder. He forced himself out of sleep and pulled the warm blanket off him. The chill of the morning air hit him and he had a strong desire just to pull the coverlet back and exchange the bedwarmth for that still nagging bladder. As he wrestled with this major decision of the morning, he was suddenly aware of a rumbling noise outside. And the sound grew. And then his room began to shake.

Rogers Kennison had lived in southern California enough years to know what was happening. Earthquake!

He rolled out of bed as the shaking increased, windows rattling, crashes in the other room as brickabrack hit the floor. He headed for the doorway—he remembered it was supposed to be a safe place—at least for the moment. He got there none too soon. Across the floor his bureau seemed to walk and he watched, amazed, as it crashed onto the bed where he had just been lying.

Gerald Schiller's new novel begins as Los Angeles shakes. His characters: Denise Burton, Rogers Kennison, Marcus Kominsky, will again find themselves enmeshed in a bizarre series of events that are part of an intricate and insidious plan that soon involves them in high level deceit and murder. These ordinary people—almost against their wishes—become caught up in some highly extraordinary events.

This exciting new novel will be available soon from InterContinental Publishing

Murder in Amsterdam
Baantjer

The two very first "DeKok" stories for the first time in a single volume, containing *DeKok and the Sunday Strangler* and *DeKok and the Corpse on Christmas Eve.*

First American edition of these European Best-Sellers in a single volume.

ISBN 1 881164 00 4

From critical reviews of **Murder in Amsterdam**:

If there could be another Maigret-like police detective, he might well be Detective-Inspector DeKok of the Amsterdam police. Similarities to Simenon abound in any critical judgement of Baantjer's work (*Bruce Cassiday*, **International Association of Crime Writers**); The two novellas make an irresistible case for the popularity of the Dutch author. DeKok's maverick personality certainly makes him a compassionate judge of other outsiders and an astute analyst of antisocial behavior (*Marilyn Stasio*, **The New York Times Book Review**); Both stories are very easy to take (**Kirkus Reviews**); Inspector DeKok is part Columbo, part Clouseau, part genius, and part imp. Baantjer has managed to create a figure hapless and honorable, bozoesque and brilliant, but most importantly, a body for whom the reader finds compassion (*Steven Rosen*, **West Coast Review of Books**); Readers of this book will understand why the author is so popular in Holland. His DeKok is a complex, fascinating individual (*Ray Browne*, **CLUES: A Journal of Detection**); This first translation of Baantjer's work into English supports the mystery writer's reputation in his native Holland as a Dutch Conan Doyle. His knowledge of esoterica rivals that of Holmes, but Baantjer wisely uses such trivia infrequently, his main interests clearly being detective work, characterization and moral complexity (**Publishers Weekly**);

ALSO FROM INTERCONTINENTAL PUBLISHING:

TENERIFE! (ISBN 1-881164-51-9 / $7.95) by Elsinck: A swiftly paced, hard-hitting story. Not for the squeamish. But nevertheless, a compelling read, written in the short take technique of a hard-sell TV commercial with whole scenes viewed in one- and two-second shots, and no pauses to catch the breath (*Bruce Cassiday*, **International Association of Crime Writers**); A fascinating work combining suspense and the study of a troubled mind to tell a story that compels the reader to continue reading (*Mac Rutherford*, **Lucky Books**); This first effort by Elsinck gives testimony to the popularity of his subsequent books. This contemporary thriller pulls no punches. A nail-biter, full of European suspense (**The Book Reader**).*

MURDER BY FAX (ISBN 1-881164-52-7 / $7.95) by Elsinck: Elsinck has created a technical tour-de-force. This high-tech version of the epistolary novel succeeds as the faxed messages quickly prove capable of providing plot, clues and characterization (**Publishers Weekly**); This novel by Dutch author Elsinck is so interestingly written it might be read for its creative style alone. It is sharp and concise and one easily becomes involved enough to read it in one sitting. MURDER BY FAX cannot help but have its American readers fall under the spell of this highly original author (*Paulette Kozick*, **West Coast Review of Books**); This clever and breezy thriller is a fun exercise. Elsinck's spirit of inventiveness keeps you guessing up to the satisfying end (*Timothy Hunter*, **[Cleveland] Plain Dealer**); The use of modern technology is nothing new, but Dutch writer Elsinck takes it one step further (*Peter Handel*, **San Francisco Chronicle**).

CONFESSION OF A HIRED KILLER (ISBN 1-881164-53-5 / $8.95) by Elsinck: Elsinck saves a nice surprise, despite its wild farrago of murder and assorted intrigue (**Kirkus Reviews**); Reading Elsinck is like peeling an onion. Once you have pulled away one layer, you'll find an even more intriguing scenario. (*Paulette Kozick*, **Rapport**) Elsinck remains a valuable asset to the thriller genre. He is original, writes in a lively style and researches his material with painstaking care (*de Volkskrant*, **Amsterdam**).

---

* Contains graphic descriptions of explicit sex and violence.

VENGEANCE: Prelude to Saddam's War
by Bob Mendes

Shocking revelations concerning his past move Michel Moreels, a Belgian industrial agent and consultant, to go to work for the Israeli Mossad. His assignment is to infiltrate a clandestine arms project designed to transform Iraq into a major international military power. Together with his girlfriend, Anna Steiner, he travels to Baghdad and succeeds in winning the trust of Colonel Saddiq Qazzaz, an officer of the *Mukhabarat*, the dreaded Iraqi Secret Police. At the risk of his own life and that of Anna, he penetrates the network of the illegal international arms trade, traditionally based in Brussels and the French-speaking part of Belgium. He meets American scientist Gerald Bull, a ballistic expert. Gradually it becomes clear to Michel that neither Bull, nor Anna, are what they appear to be. The more he learns about international secret services and the people who are determined to manipulate him, the more his Iraqi mission takes on a personal character: one of Vengeance!

A "faction-thriller" based on actual events in Iraq and Western Europe.
A Bertelsmann (Europe) Book Club Selection.
First American edition of this European Best-Seller.

ISBN 1-881164-71-3 **($9.95)**

Bob Mendes is the winner of the (1993) "Gouden Strop" (Golden Noose). The "Golden Noose" is an annual award given to the best thriller or crime/spy novel published in the Dutch language. "An intelligent and convincing intrigue in fast tempo; in writing *Vengeance*, Bob Mendes has produced a thriller of international allure." **(From the Jury's report for the Golden Noose, 1993)** . . . Compelling and well-documented—Believable—a tremendously exciting thriller—a powerful visual ability—compelling, tension–filled and extremely well written—rivetting action and finely detailed characters—smooth transition from fact to fiction and back again . . . **(a sampling of Dutch and Flemish reviews).**

ALSO FROM INTERCONTINENTAL PUBLISHING:

The "DeKok" series by Baantjer.

If there could be another Maigret-like police detective, he might well be Detective-Inspector DeKok of the Amsterdam police. Similarities to Simenon abound in any critical judgement of Baantjer's work (**Bruce Cassiday, International Association of Crime Writers**); DeKok's maverick personality certainly makes him a compassionate judge of other outsiders and an astute analyst of antisocial behavior (**Marilyn Stasio, The New York Times Book Review**); DeKok is part Columbo, part Clouseau, part genius, and part imp. (**Steven Rosen, West Coast Review of Books**); It's easy to understand the appeal of Amsterdam police detective DeKok (**Charles Solomon, Los Angeles Times**); DeKok is a careful, compassionate policeman in the tradition of Maigret (**Library Journal**); This series is the answer to an insomniac's worst fears (**Robin W. Winks, The Boston Globe**).

The following Baantjer/DeKok books are currently in print:

MURDER IN AMSTERDAM (contains complete text of *DeKok and the Sunday Strangler* and *DeKok and the Corpse on Christmas Eve*);
DEKOK AND THE SOMBER NUDE
DEKOK AND THE DEAD HARLEQUIN
DEKOK AND THE SORROWING TOMCAT
DEKOK AND THE DISILLUSIONED CORPSE
DEKOK AND THE CAREFUL KILLER
DEKOK AND THE ROMANTIC MURDER
DEKOK AND THE DYING STROLLER
DEKOK AND THE CORPSE AT THE CHURCH WALL
DEKOK AND THE DANCING DEATH
DEKOK AND THE NAKED LADY
DEKOK AND THE BROTHERS OF THE EASY DEATH
DEKOK AND THE DEADLY ACCORD
DEKOK AND MURDER IN SEANCE
DEKOK AND MURDER ON THE MENU.

Available soon: **DeKok and Murder in Ecstacy; DeKok and the Begging Death; DeKok and the Geese of Death** and more ...
Additional titles published regularly.

Available in your bookstore. U.S. distribution by IPG, Chicago, IL.

DU